Changing Seasons

Endorsements

Watching a loved one slip into dementia is one of the most difficult situations to endure. In *Changing Seasons*, Nora must navigate her grief over watching her father slip away and a breakup with her longtime boyfriend. Sue A. Fairchild takes us through the myriad of emotions with grace and hope. In this moving story, she shows us that it is never too late to embrace change.
—**Jane Daly** author of *Where Is My Sister*

In *Changing Seasons*, author Sue A. Fairchild has captured the essence of dealing with family members and their long goodbye as they struggle with dementia. Add to this, characters seeking their own purpose in life through the use of their God-given talents, and you have a story that is gripping and relatable. For those of us with friends and/or family members facing the struggle against dementia and Alzheimer's, the story rings true. Yet Fairchild's writing presents a side of the story that is full of hope, comfort, and life.
—**Janet L. Pierce**, PhD and devotional and historical fiction writer.

If you're walking through a season of change (like most of us) and are questioning God along your journey—seeking answers on a relationship, a project or purpose, your faith, your future—Nora's story in *Changing Seasons* will not only resonate with you but tug at your heartstrings and give you hope you're not alone—and you will find the answers.
—**Michele Chynoweth**, bestselling author of the novel, *The Jealous Son*, now being made into a major motion picture.

Sue Fairchild hooks you from the first page of *Changing Seasons,* a heartfelt novel exploring finding purpose when life feels upside down. Through the slow, painful journey of dementia and the complexities of singlehood and dating relationships, Fairchild masterfully reveals the hope in the Father's guiding hand, showing how He works good in every season of life.

—**Cheryl Pelton Lutz,** author of the award-winning *Securely Held: Finding Significance and Security in the Shelter of God's Embrace.*

Sue Fairchild has done it again. *Changing Seasons,* her follow up to *Changing Tides,* is another carefully crafted, beautiful story. It follows the character, Nora, from the first book on her journey to find her purpose in life. Fairchild does not shy away from difficult topics like loss and dementia, but somehow makes reading about these struggles palatable. Her likable characters and attention to the details of action, description, and emotion drew me in right from the first page. The connections her characters make with each other and with God are powerful. I look forward to reading her next book.

—**Linda Foster Tripp**, author of *Annie and the Healing Box*

Full of heartache and hope, Fairchild's second book sweeps you into the relatable life and struggles of a woman trying to figure out what's next. A heart-tugging, heart-warming, spirit-stirring book.

—**Karin Beery**, multi-award-winning author

Changing Seasons

SUE A. FAIRCHILD

Copyright Notice

Cover and Interior Design: Kelly Artieri, Deb Haggerty
Editor(s): Cristel Phelps, Deb Haggerty

PUBLISHED BY: Elk Lake Publishing, Inc., 35 Dogwood Drive, Plymouth, MA 02360, 2024

Library Cataloging Data
Names: Fairchild, Sue A. (Sue A. Fairchild)
Changing Seasons / Sue A. Fairchild
214 p. 23cm × 15cm (9in × 6 in.)

Changing Seasons

ISBN-13: 9798891342620 (paperback) | 9798891342637 (trade paperback) | 9798891342644 (e-book)

Key Words: dementia caregivers, Alzheimer's, caregiving elderly parents, seeking God's purpose, photography, family crisis, small town siblings

Library of Congress Control Number: 2024947772 Fiction

Dedication

To my readers who loved my other book so much,
they wanted more.

Acknowledgments

First and foremost, I want to thank God for providing this gift of writing. When I set out to write Nora's story, I really had no clue where she was really from or what her issues were. I've gone through many rewrites, but God knew where this story needed to go and placed people, readers, in my path to help. Without God, I would not have become a writer, I wouldn't have finished this story, and this book wouldn't be in your hands right now. Praise be to God.

Thank you, as always, to my writer's group, the West Branch Christian Writers, for all their support, input, and love. Especially Bev Wert who works with Alzheimer patients and gave me a wealth of feedback and guidance. She's writing her own book about caregiving to Alzheimer patients that you need to read when it's published.

Thank you to Tracy Cooper, Crystal Hayduk, and Jill Thomas, who have been more than friends—they are sisters in Christ in this crazy writing life. You all have kept me on task with this book but also kept my mind focused on God in the process—a task more important than writing. And when I'm feeling that old imposter syndrome kick in, you remind me who I am and whose I am.

Thanks to my friends at Elk Lake Publishing. I truly love the family Deb Haggerty has created there and am honored to be published by this fine Christian publisher.

I also want to acknowledge friends and acquaintances who filled in some gaps about dealing with family members with dementia. I have not experienced this, so their personal stories, insights, and feedback helped shaped this book in a tangible way. I used a lot of what these folks told me, especially about the nursing home setting and how patients deal in different ways.

Finally, thanks to my husband, John, who has dealt with dementia in his family to a small extent. I pray we will never experience this awful disease because I never want to forget all your love for me. I love you and am so blessed by your daily encouragement and love. Without you (and your job), I would probably not have this life of making my own hours, setting my own goals, and living the life God meant for me. But he gave me you in order to accomplish it all, and I'm so glad he did.

Chapter One

Nora threw her bag down on the couch and walked to the fridge for a soda. The drive back from the Outer Banks had been long, and she just wanted to crawl into bed and sleep. Maybe she could hold off returning to her real world for another few hours.

The sound of work boots pounding up the wooden front porch steps erased all hopes of that. The squeak of the screen door was followed by more heavy footfalls through the house.

How did he know I was home already?

She turned, with soda can in hand, to look at her brother.

"Where have you been? You've been gone for a week."

"Is that how long it's been? Felt shorter ..." Nora popped the top of the can of soda and brought it to her mouth, relishing the ping of the fizz on her lip.

Dell stood with his hands on his hips and glared, waiting for her real reply. They had played this game as kids too. As the younger sister, she often didn't answer him to his liking, but he would wait. He had that gift—the gift of patience. She didn't.

She sipped a drop of soda from the lid, then sighed. "Delbert Harper, don't get your knickers in a twist. I'm home now."

She knew he hated being called by his full, proper name, but she needed to establish the upper hand somehow as the younger sister—she forty-one and he about to turn forty-four. Being away for the week had probably sent him into a tizzy. She should have told him she was going. Or where she was. Or when she'd planned to be back. Or answered the multiple text messages he had sent her. Or answered his phone calls.

But that was all water under the bridge now.

"You're not funny, Nor. I thought you might be dead. You could've, at least, answered one text." Dell held up a finger to punctuate his point. "What do you think we thought?" The finger went back down, and he slapped his pant leg with the hand. "You could've been abducted for all I knew!"

Doubtful. No one wanted ... needed her that badly.

"I know Jill told you where I was."

Dell had begun to pace her hardwood floors now, the old wood shifting and creaking as he went. He ran a hand through his brown hair. Thinning, she noticed. Finally, he stopped to face her again.

"Life went on just the same this past week while you were gone, by the way. Not that you asked."

Ah, switching tactics.

"You didn't give me the chance to ask, Dell." She pushed herself away from the counter and brushed past him back into the living room. "You came in here all hot and bothered before I even had a chance to catch my breath."

Her cottage was small but comfortable. Only one story and five rooms, the home had served her purposes for the past three years but now felt a little too claustrophobic with her brother breathing down her neck. Dell followed at her heels as she diverted out to the porch.

Need some air.

Dell followed her there too, the screen door slapping back into place behind him.

"And if life went on fine without me, what's the issue?" she called over her shoulder.

She went to the porch swing and sat with one leg tucked under herself. She took another sip of her soda—wishing it was mixed with something—as she looked out across the front lawn. Down the lane about a half mile was her brother's house, sitting next to her father's. But their father hadn't lived in his own home for several weeks. He lived with Dell and his family now. Nora choked on the lump in her throat and took another sip of her soda to wash it away.

Dell paced the wooden porch floor in front of her now. "Dad needs you. He's been asking about you all week, and I didn't know what to tell him."

A flush of guilt rose in her throat as she watched him pace for a bit. "Dell, sit down before you give me a headache. I just had a very long car drive, and I don't need this right now."

Her brother glared at her once more before plopping down beside her. The swing bent and swayed with his weight, and she had to brace herself against the arm to keep from being toppled off.

"Well, since I had no idea where you were, I'm sorry I can't be more accommodating to your reentry into the real world." Dell pushed at the porch floor with one foot, setting the swing in motion.

"Jill *did* tell you, didn't she?" Nora turned to glare at him.

Dell glanced at her. "Yes." He blew out a burst of air in a loud sigh. "But Dad has been getting worse, and you just left me. And I'm handling all the stuff at the funeral home too. I needed to talk to you at the very least."

Dell and their father had always taken care of the funeral home without her ... until Daddy's dementia had started to show and worsen. Now she was working at the funeral home, which she hated, and Dell was taking care of more things—like moving their father into his home when he'd left the stove on one too many times.

She'd tried to help, obtaining her mortician's license last year. But Daddy kept insisting he didn't need help, and Nora didn't love the business anyway, so she never tried very hard. The place was morbid, dark, and gloomy—the old Victorian funeral home reeked of death.

But she knew just running off had been the wrong thing to do, and yet ... she had needed the break. She longed for some adventure, some new scenery. And her time in the Outer Banks—OBX to those in the know—had been just what she needed. Refreshing. Enlightening.

She had even made a new friend. She sipped her soda and thought of Gabe, hoping he would respond when she texted him later. In fact, she should text him now, tell him she had returned home safely. Patting her pants pocket, she realized she'd left her phone inside. She didn't want Dell to linger, so she sat still, hoping he would get out his anger and return to his family so she could sleep.

"Jake has been looking for you too, ya know." Her brother looked at her and she frowned.

She sighed. She'd only texted Jake that she'd be gone for a week. He'd simply texted back "K." Why hadn't her fiancé been more worried about her like her brother had been?

She and Jake had been on again off again in a committed relationship for close to ten years, but something just never felt ... right. They'd been planning their wedding. Again. This time, though, she'd agreed to a date in May. But as she'd begun to look at invitations and dresses, she'd felt sick. A queasiness she couldn't shake—until she'd run to the beach.

It wouldn't be the first time she'd called off a possible wedding with Jake. But they'd gotten back together so many times. Started over, time and again. What was wrong with her? Why couldn't she commit? Jake had always wanted marriage, but Nora had wanted adventure. To get out of Millsburgh and see the world. To find her purpose. Small town life fit Jake like a glove but made Nora feel trapped.

She knew she'd probably cancel their wedding again. Perhaps Jake would finally move on from her this time instead of trying to make their relationship work. Maybe this would be his tipping point. She sipped again at her soda, again wishing the cola was something stronger.

Dell sighed beside her. "I can tell by the lack of response that you might not care about Jake at this point, right? So, what's going on?"

Just feeling trapped in a world not of my own making. No biggie.

"I can't settle down. Can you hear that word? Settle. I don't want to settle, Dell. I want to find my purpose. My person ... if there is one. A place of my own in this world. Not trapped in a business I hate and being married to a man I've *settled* for." She blew out a hot breath. "I pick fights with Jake about everything. And he didn't understand Dad moving in with you. He thought we should just put him in a home. Can you imagine?" She scoffed. "And if I'm going to have someone in my life, I want that someone to understand me and my family. Someone that being with feels ... right. Like you with Natalie." She took a deep breath this time. "I can't love Jake like he loves me."

Life, in fact, had been pretty miserable this last year. She had gone a little bit crazy with everything happening, in truth—some of the reasons she had wanted to get away for a bit. The other being to avoid Jake and talk about weddings. When her friend Jill offered her beach house in the OBX as a place to get away, Nora didn't hesitate. She had packed her bags with the speed of a racing locomotive and left town before anyone could stop her.

"You've been a bit unmoored since Mom died."

"I've been unmoored since well before that, big brother. I don't feel like I've ever found my place in this world. Something to call my own. I thought helping more with the business would help, but I remembered the morbidity of it. I had to get away. I know you don't understand. And I'm sorry I didn't let you know. I just needed to try and figure myself out." Her soda can now empty, she picked at the tab, making a pinging sound that rippled out into the late afternoon air.

Dell nodded. "I kind of figured that was what happened. Jill told me after a few days where you had gone. Made me promise not to come get you. Good thing North Carolina is quite the hike from Pennsylvania." He narrowed his eyes at her. "I wouldn't mind getting away too, ya know. Could have taken me with you."

Heat flushed her cheeks as she realized Dell was just as worn down as she. When their father's dementia had started a few years ago after their mother died, they never imagined things would get this hard. Now Dell had to work to keep up their family's business and two houses while his younger sister just flitted away when things got too hard.

"So did you?"

Nora looked at her brother. "Did I what?"

"Figure yourself out."

She snorted. "Nope. Might be even more confused, in fact."

"Well, at least there was sun."

Dell set the swing into motion again, and a few minutes passed in silence.

When her thoughts began to get the best of her again as they often did, she asked, "Anyone die while I was gone?"

Dead people wait, she knew, but families often didn't, and she needed to take over as the face of Harper Funeral Home now. Since Daddy had never included her in the behind-the-scenes work, she now did the public relations bits—meeting with families, signing contracts, setting up obituaries, and running the actual funerals—while Dell did the stuff she couldn't stomach.

"You were lucky. Not a single one. Although, old man Hoffmaster is supposedly not doing well. You should call his granddaughter Sarah soon."

She nodded. "I'll do it tomorrow."

A few more moments passed in silence until Dell bumped her shoulder with his own.

"The kids missed you."

She arched an eyebrow at him. "But not you, huh?"

Dell smirked. "I missed coming over here and eating your snacks. Does that count?"

"Nope."

"Well, ... Katie cried for almost two days straight thinking you would never come back. Feeling guilty yet?"

A little.

"I'm sorry. I'll apologize to her tomorrow." She loved her brother's kids and his wife, Natalie. *At least I won't be totally alone when Dad dies.* "If you need to get away, I'll cover for you. For one week only." She put her index finger in his face.

He swatted her away and said, "Nah. I'm a big, strong man. I no have feelings." He slouched like a caveman and scratched his protruding brow with a knuckle.

She poked him in the stomach, and he blew out a burst of air and laughed. Then he swung his arm over her shoulder and pulled her close.

"Yes, I missed you, you dumb bunny. And don't ever leave me again."

"Can't promise you anything. Besides you have that beautiful wife and four great kids. You don't need me."

"Of course I do. And they do too. This is where you belong."

She didn't know about that. She didn't seem to fit in here. Not even with the work at her family's funeral home, which she hated. But she'd never found another job where she fit in either. And she'd done a lot of jobs—cashier, waitress, bank clerk—none of them had ever fulfilled her.

"Pretty sure you could run the business without me," she told him.

"Nah. Where would the fun be in that?" Her brother snorted, kissed the top of her head, then stood from the swing. "Welcome home. I have to get home for dinner. Natalie is probably worried sick. When I saw your car drive up the lane, I barreled out the door like a man on a mission. Surprised my phone's not ringing yet."

His words seemed to predict the future as his cell phone started to ring inside his pocket. Once more she thought of texting her new friend Gabe.

Why am I not thinking about texting Jake?

"You better get moving," she said.

He smiled as he stepped off the porch, avoiding all three steps. "If you need food, you know where to get some. Otherwise, I'll see you tomorrow. When there will still be food if you get hungry."

Tomorrow ... she didn't want to think about that yet.

Chapter Two

The next morning, Nora took Dell up on his food offer and ate breakfast with his brood. Natalie pulled her into an embrace the minute she saw Nora at the door, then ushered her to the kitchen and started plopping food in front of her as the kids gathered around for hugs.

"Aunt Nora! You back. I missed you." Five-year-old Katie crawled into Nora's lap and patted her cheek.

"Yes, string bean, I'm home. I'm sorry I worried you. How are these three brothers treating you?"

Katie was the youngest of Dell's four kids and the only girl. Brett age six, Ethan "almost eight," and Mason nine going on twenty were her brothers. Mason had given her a quick hug around the waist before going to get ready for church, while the other two boys sat next to her and peppered her with questions.

"Where did you go?"

"Did you drive the whole way?"

"Weren't you scared to go alone?"

She answered all their questions calmly around bites of eggs, bacon, and toast. When her plate was finally clean—and she had waved Natalie off from serving her more—she kissed Katie on the cheek and said, "Okay, brats. That's enough. You all better get ready for church."

Katie said, "I already has my dress on. See?" She leaned back so Nora could see. She did, indeed, already have on a dress.

"And Dad isn't back yet," chimed in Ethan.

Dell often picked up odd jobs here and there with the neighbors. It was his "Christian duty," he'd said. Although he never asked for money, folks usually shoved a twenty or more into his hands for the work.

This morning, Dell had gone down to Mr. Hoffmaster's home to help Sarah's husband move in a hospital bed for the old man. The hospital was sending him home this week, where he wished to die.

Dell always fit in everywhere—in high school he had the larger pack of friends, at the funeral home he was Dad's right-hand-man, and the community loved him like their own son. Nora had never found her niche the way he had.

"You come to church too?" Katie asked, snuggling her head into Nora's neck.

"I'm not sure, baby girl. I might be needed elsewhere."

"We could stay home and play a video game, Aunt Nora," Ethan said. He bounced down off his chair and ran for the living room. "I'll show you the one I just got."

"Not today, buddy!" she called.

She could hear his disappointed flop to the floor, but a moment later the strained sounds of a video game.

"Don't worry," Natalie said, "He'll forget all about you joining him in a minute ... if he hasn't already." Natalie lifted her youngest from Nora's lap and gave her a squeeze. "You might be dressed appropriately, Katie, but that tangled hair needs to be dealt with. Why don't you go into your room and pick out a pretty bow, and I'll come in a minute to sort it all out?" When Katie began to protest, she said, "Aunt Nora will be here when you get back." She turned to Nora with raised eyebrows. "Right?"

She guessed she deserved that. "Yes." When Katie ran off to her room, Nora said, "I thought I'd stay with Dad while you were at church today."

Natalie said, "I thought maybe you'd want to come to church and see Jake."

Nora put her dish in the sink and sighed. She'd need to deal with him sooner or later, but she preferred later. "I just thought you'd need help with Dad today. And I need to call Sarah later and do some paperwork."

Natalie sat down and gave Nora a pointed look, telling her to sit down too. She did.

"What's going on with you? First you run off, now you're avoiding Jake and church. That's not like you, Nora."

Nora pulled apart a napkin left on the table. "I know. When I was looking at the wedding invitations last week the whole thing just didn't seem ... it didn't seem right, ya know? Jake's all hyped up about the wedding and talking about getting a bigger house, maybe moving ... kids. I'm forty-one! I'll be almost forty-two by the time we wed in May. I'm not sure kids are in the mix for me at this stage. And Dad ..."

As if on cue, her father walked into the room holding a plate. "That boy in the other room is playing those loud games again, Natalie." He held out an empty plate to his daughter-in-law. "I found this on the coffee table."

Natalie took the plate from him and walked it to the sink. "You wanted to eat in the living room, Dad. This was your plate. And Ethan is allowed to play games before church." She turned back to him. "Nora said she'd stay with you this morning if you don't want to go to church."

Nora knew his answer would be determined more on if he remembered what "going to church" meant, but she stayed quiet, hoping not to confuse him further.

Nora's father looked down at himself, at the pajama bottoms he still wore, and scowled. "I don't think this is right."

"Well, you got the shirt right." Natalie smiled.

He'd somehow remembered the button-down shirt and tie ... but not the pants.

Natalie moved to him, put her hands on his shoulders, and turned him in the direction of the guest room off the kitchen. "Your church pants are hanging in the closet. I'll be in to help you."

Her father walked away, grumbling about being bossed around.

Natalie turned back to Nora. "I'm starting to think I have five kids."

"Six if you count Dell." Nora smiled.

Natalie laughed. "Sometimes." She returned to her seat beside Nora. "But having someone to share all this chaos with helps too."

Nora sighed. "I know. I want that too. I just ... Jake's not the one. I keep thinking he is. Or I guess I think he's the only option. If I don't marry him, I'll die alone. But when stuff started to happen with Dad, I couldn't see him holding me up, ya know? He just kept talking about what he called 'fun' stuff—vacations, new houses—I don't think I can handle all that change right now, nor do I think we should be doing a bunch of fun things when Dad is obviously getting worse."

"Not sure you can pin all this on Dad," Natalie said with a raised eyebrow. "Don't you love him?"

"Of course I love Dad. That's what I'm—"

"Jake, Nora. Do you love *Jake*?"

Nora opened her mouth to respond, but wanting to get the words right, she shut it again. Finally, she said, "I thought I did, but when I met this guy last week, I realized maybe I just love Jake because he loves me. I want to be with him so I'm not lonely in my old age. That isn't the same as being in love. Is it?"

Natalie shook her head. "It's not. When it's right, you'll know, trust me. You should talk to Jake about all of this. He'll understand. You guys have been together so long, and I doubt he would want you to marry him just to avoid loneliness."

Nora continued to shred the napkin into tiny pieces. "I'm not sure. Although, it's not fair to keep stringing Jake along either."

Natalie reached out for her hand. "He's been asking Dell about you. I think he loves you, Nora, and you should at least talk with him."

Nora's father called from the other room. "I can't find my shirt!"

Natalie rose and started for the guest room. "You had your shirt on already, Dad. Just the pants. You should come to church with us," she said over her shoulder to Nora. "He's coming with us so that negates your excuse."

"But Jake will still be there."

"You can't avoid him forever. Best to get the whole thing over with."

Nora nodded as she started to do the dishes piled up in the sink.

Natalie called out to her from down the hallway. "We have a dishwasher for that!"

Sighing, Nora wiped her hands on a kitchen towel, then looked around for another task. Finding none—*curse Natalie and her organized ways*—she trudged to the front room.

Ethan sat on the couch, playing his video on a small screen.

"Hey little man, are you ready for church?"

Ethan looked up and nodded. "Promise to play later?" His eyes lit up once more. "I can show you the new dinosaur Dad got me. It roars and everything."

He began to climb down from the couch, but Nora stopped him.

"Wait. Yes, but later. We'll be leaving for church soon."

Ethan slumped back onto the couch and stared at his game, saying nothing.

Nora patted the little blond head and moved to the front door.

She looked up the lane to her house. The leaves had just started to turn, as September wound into October. North Carolina was nice, but she could never move there like Gabe had. She would miss the changing seasons, especially fall, in Pennsylvania. This stretch of road had plenty of trees to watch the foliage shift every autumn.

She thought of all the leaves covering her front lawn and the back-breaking work cleaning them all up every year too.

"Well, can't have everything," she mused.

Chapter Three

Nora sat next to little Katie in the pew as other families filtered in around them. Her father sat on the other side of Katie, his hand holding hers. Katie chattered away to her grandfather while he sat still, looking forward. The scene reminded Nora of her own self as a youngster, holding her father's hand and chattering away, even after he'd hush her at the beginning of the service.

Natalie sat next to her with the boys while Dell sat on the other side of their father. "Hemming him in," Dell had said. He'd taken to getting up in the middle of the service and trying to wander off.

As the organist ended her prelude, the last of the people took their seats. A few moments later, they all stood again to sing the first hymn.

Nora loved their church with its adherence to old traditions. Although they incorporated some modern praise songs, they still sang the old standards from hymnals. Church was one place Nora felt moored, stable. If only she could find this peace outside these walls.

Pastor Richfield stood as the congregation sat, moving to the pulpit to begin his sermon. He began by reading from Ecclesiastes.

"'To everything there is a season, A time for every purpose under heaven ...'"

A time for every purpose under heaven. But what is my purpose? When is my time?

"'He has made everything beautiful in its time',"Pastor Richfield continued. "'Also He has put eternity in their hearts, except that no one can find out the work that God does from beginning to end. I know that nothing is better for them than to rejoice, and to do good in their lives.' In some translations, this last verse says 'to be happy and to do good'.'"

Nora thought about this last bit. "To be happy and to do good." What good was she doing?

"Now some of you might think this verse means we should never be sad, and we all need to be missionaries." A small bit of nervous laughter echoed about the room. "Well, it does, and it doesn't. We often think about missionaries in other countries, living in squalid, dusty, poor conditions. But your mission field could be right in front of you. A mission could be helping your neighbor or teaching young children. Maybe your season is changing. Maybe you've been a teacher a long time, and now are retired but feel a sense of loss. Where is your purpose now?"

Is he speaking directly to me today?

"Search your heart, talk to God. He knows your purpose, the life he wants you to live for him. Ask him about your gifts and his purpose for your life. Listen to the small voice leading you. Do good while you yet live."

Pastor Richfield ended his sermon, and the congregation rose again to sing "Make Me A Blessing." Nora sang the words and wondered how she might be a blessing to others.

I don't feel content, Lord. I don't feel fulfilled or ... happy as your verse says. What am I doing wrong?

❦ ❦ ❦ ❦ ❦

In the parking lot after the service, Nora had avoided Jake and made her way outside to wait on Dell and his family. She watched as people she'd known for many years shook the pastor's hand and walked to their cars. Some nodded her way and smiled, but none came to talk with her.

Dell, on the other hand, held court with a group of men at the base of the church steps. Her brother smiled and smacked the backs of several men. After the exchange, she watched as they bowed their heads in prayer for one another. What she wouldn't give for a group like that of her own.

When the men broke apart, she noticed Jake standing next to her brother. They chatted for a moment before looking over at her. Jake smiled, and she felt her heart flipflop. He was a good-looking man—tall with dark hair and striking blue eyes. When he patted her brother on the shoulder and began walking her way, she looked about for a place to hide.

Get a hold of yourself. He's already seen you, dummy.

"Hey, Jake. What's up?"

"Hey, you look tan."

Jake laughed, and her heart did a little flutter again.

Knock it off, heart, we've made our decision. I think.

He leaned in for a kiss.

She turned her head, so his lips fell on her cheek.

"Gees, I thought my fiancée would want a kiss after being apart for a whole week." He put his arm around her waist and tried to pull her close, but she resisted until he stopped and stepped away. "Okay, that's how we're going to play it. Fine. When did you get back? I thought you'd call me."

Now he stood with hands on his hips, glaring down at her. She felt guilty for not just pretending everything was okay. For not simply playing the game they always played. But not doing so felt good, somehow.

There is nothing better for people than to be happy ...

She took a deep breath and let it out through her nose before replying. "I wasn't ready to talk. We *need* to talk but not here and not now."

"Yes, I need to talk with you about an idea I've had."

"Again, I don't think this is the time. I just got back late last night, and I need to do laundry and have some stuff at the funeral home to deal with."

Jake sighed. "Fine. But I'll be out of town for a few days."

"Where are you going?"

"Up to Vermont. Dad needs me to talk to some people up there." She nodded and he continued. "How about dinner when I get back? We can go out—neutral territory."

She debated the idea. Going out would offer a public place to end their relationship ... once and for all. Perhaps if others were a witness, she'd not be weak and return to him as she had time and again. But the moment would be out in the open ... for everyone to see if they had an argument.

"I don't know, Jake, I think—"

"I just want to have dinner with one of the prettiest girls in Millsburgh. My fiancée."

"Woman." The word came out of her mouth without a thought.

Jake frowned. "What?"

"I'm not a girl, Jake. I'm in my forties, own my own home. I think that gives me the right to be called a woman."

Am I trying to convince him or me?

He sighed, and Nora felt a twinge of regret.

Why are you being this way?

She pressed away the rational part of her mind.

She knew she was just trying to rationalize the decision she'd made in her head, but not yet told Jake—that they were done. Finally and for good. Maybe she should just tell him now. Dell and his family were now waiting for her by their car.

"Fine, I want to have dinner with one of the prettiest *women* in Millsburgh. No, wait. *The* prettiest woman in town. Okay?" Jake sighed. "Just say yes. We can chat about the wedding and make honeymoon plans and I can tell you about my idea."

"What idea?" she asked.

"It's not a done deal yet, so you'll have to wait. But if you say you'll have dinner with me when I get back, I'll tell you then." He stepped closer again and put his arm around her waist. "I'll take you anywhere you want to go. Even that Indian place you love so much."

He had lowered his voice to that tone he knew she couldn't resist. Sexy, sultry ... *ugh*. And offering to go anywhere she wanted had always been one of his ploys when he wanted something in return. She wouldn't fall for it. Why would she? She had no need of Jake Marshall anymore. She was going to move on, and she should tell him. And yet ... she did love that Indian place.

Chapter Four

After lunch with Dell and his family, Nora drove downtown to the funeral home. The imposing building had originally been the home of her great-great-grandfather and his family. He'd built the house in the Queen Anne style—with a wraparound porch, asymmetrical façade, classical columns, and round tower—as a home and business. There was still a small carriage house in the back that housed a very old funeral carriage. They sometimes carted the ornate, large-wheeled hearse out for parades and special events. Over the years, the Harpers had bought or built other homes for their families away from the business and now utilized the upper floors for storage.

Her dad had made many changes to the building during his lifetime, including an accessible ramp, sturdier railings, and an elevator to the second floor. But the exterior style and the interior furnishings had been kept in the Victorian style, the warm wood tones, ornate floral wallpaper, and curved lines comforting to the bereaved. They even had one room with a cozy little fireplace they lit during winter funerals.

"When someone dies, a person needs warm things," her father had often said.

As Nora unlocked the door to their business—jiggling the ages-old key to gain purchase—she heard the phone on her desk ringing. She ran to answer it, noticing the red light blinking, indicating several messages were waiting. She really needed to figure out how to connect this thing to her cell.

"Harper Funeral Services, how can I help you?" she answered, slightly out of breath.

Her father had told her they needed to answer whenever the phone rang. Death did not only occur during normal business hours.

"Nora? This is Sarah Anderson ... Bud Hoffmaster's granddaughter?"

Oh no. She'd meant to call Sarah today, but the task had slipped her mind. She thought of how Dell had just helped move Mr. Hoffmaster's bed. Were his efforts all for nothing?

"Yes, Sarah. How are you ... how is your grandfather?" Nora winced. Her father had taught her not to ask that question, but the query just came naturally.

"Asking often upsets people," he'd told her. "Especially since they're usually calling because their loved one has died."

She would never get the hang of this business.

"He's stable and at home now," Sarah said in her ear. "Dell said you were going to call, and I know you were away and probably just getting back in the swing, but ... well, I was wondering if you would come and chat with him to ensure we have everything ready for ... um ..."

Most people had trouble saying the words. Nora broke in to relieve her of the task.

"Absolutely. I intended to call today, but you beat me to it." No sense Sarah knowing her mind slip. "Let me just check my calendar ..." She moved papers around to reveal the paper calendar they kept on the desk, even though she knew there was nothing on it. "I can stop by tomorrow morning. Would that work? Say ten o'clock? I do think your father has set up some things, but I'll need to look over his file first."

She heard Sarah let out a breath. "Yes. Great. That's fine. He's a bit tired from his move today anyway. We'll see you tomorrow at ten. Thank you."

"You're welcome. See you then."

Nora hung up the phone, then sat down in the stiff leather chair behind the desk. Her father's chair. She looked around at the dark paneled walls and thought, not for the first time, how this space was her father's and not hers. Dell had said she could remodel, make the room her own, but she'd resisted. Was this where she would stay? Was this where she could "do good" as Pastor Richfield had said in his sermon? Was this job truly her purpose in life?

She didn't see how when she didn't even want to be here, talking to people about their dead relatives, helping to pick out ornate caskets that would just be put into the ground never to be seen again. The people were dead, why did they need silk fabric?

She pushed the thoughts from her head and turned to dig through her father's filing cabinet behind her. She'd been meaning to put everything into a computer file for ease of access. Although her father had kept decent records, his filing system had been haphazard at best. She had trouble finding Bud Hoffmaster's file until she remembered his real first name was Byron. She opened the folder and bits of different sized notes fell out—some things written on a sheet of legal-sized paper, and others jotted down on brightly colored Post-it notes. Bud had picked out a casket and had a plot, but she didn't see anything about the service or who would officiate. Nor had he paid for any part. Which was not unusual, although some people did pay ahead of time.

She gathered each bit of paper in a pile and began her own list on another sheet of paper. As she jotted down each item, she flung the haphazard paper into the trash can next to the desk.

I need to do this with every file in that cabinet.

Who knew how long some of these files had been set up? Maybe they needed updating too. After finishing up Bud's new file and placing it to the side for tomorrow, she pulled out another stack and made room on her desk. This could be the perfect distraction for her day.

As she shuffled through the first couple of files, she noted missing items in each. Perhaps her dad's memory and organization skills had begun to fail earlier than they thought.

She opened her laptop and started a spreadsheet.

Best to try and make sense of this.

As she input the data she had, she wished there was a better way of making sense of things. Maybe putting together packages would encourage people to pay ahead of time, keep things organized, and help their cash flow. She made a note in her phone to talk with Dell tomorrow when he came to work before moving back to the desk phone.

There were only two messages and both from Dell, trying to find her when she had been away. She erased both and sat back again in the chair.

She thought more about the package idea, took out a note pad, and began to write.

Casket / urn

Fee for funeral service

Embalming

Removal of body

She would need to come up with less blunt language. No one wanted to think about the "removal of the body." Yet people often died at home, and the body had to be removed.

Changing Seasons

Nora looked at the piled-up bills on the desk. Perhaps they needed to raise their prices too. She jotted another note about that, then turned back to the laptop on the desk to check email messages and research what other homes charged.

The emails were mostly junk, other businesses trying to sell them their services. She made another note to check with Dell to see if he knew which suppliers they currently used. Everything was too confusing to her. *How will I ever sort all of this out?* Her father had been in charge for almost five decades—he had taken over from his own father in his twenties—and knew the names and contacts of all his suppliers almost as well as he knew her and Dell.

Except now his memory was hit or miss. But maybe he'd gone over these things with Dell before his mind had started to slip.

Maybe she could ask her dad directly. She thought about how he had sometimes forgotten her name and called her Natalie. *They both start with N. Easy mix-up.* But she knew it was not so simple. The doctor had told them the lapses were indicative of dementia and would only get worse.

She turned back to the filing cabinet. Maybe she'd find more information in there. As she piled the papers on the desk, she realized just how much work there was to do and how ill-qualified she was to do it.

Chapter Five

Nora smoothed down the front of her skirt as she sat in her car in front of the Hoffmaster's house. She hated wearing skirts, but her father had often admonished her to be professional in her appearance. She doubted her normal jeans and hooded sweatshirts qualified as professional. This morning, she had dressed in a navy-blue A-line skirt with a tan sweater. Since returning from the beach, and despite the still warmish temperatures, she had felt cold.

The rear-view mirror reflected a woman beyond her years, her hair thinner—a contrast to the thick mane she'd had in her younger years. *Stress,* her friend Jill had told her. She smoothed a piece of stray bang out of her eye. She shouldn't have worn so much mascara. The sharp black accentuated the lines growing around her eyes. She rummaged in her purse for some concealer, then patted the makeup into the lines. She consulted the mirror again. *Good enough.*

She grabbed the brown leather folder with Mr. Hoffmaster's information from the passenger seat and exited the car. She touched her bun atop her head to ensure every hair was still in place—which it should be, considering how many pins she had put in there. She frowned at the tight bun. She'd have a headache for sure if she didn't let her hair out soon. *The price of professionalism.*

She tottered toward the front door on one-inch kitten heels. She hated heels too, but these were the lowest and most professional she could find. And they did make her legs look great.

Before she could knock, Sarah swung open the door and offered a smile. Her blue eyes sparkled, but Nora could see the tinge of darkness under her eyes.

"Nora, don't you look great. Come in, please." She stood aside for Nora to enter. "My youngest just spilled orange juice on my blouse so ..." She frowned, while holding a napkin to a widening dark orange spot near the left shoulder of her white T-shirt. "I forgot that moms should not wear white."

Nora chuckled. "Yes, I have heard th—"

"Mom! Where did you put the iPad?" a child yelled from another room.

"I'm so sorry. Why don't you make yourself comfortable while I go deal with this. I'll be right back," Sarah said to Nora, then closed the door and went to deal with the child. Nora could hear her reprimanding the boy for yelling.

"Nora Harper, is that you?"

She turned to see Bud Hoffmaster lying on a bed surrounded by metal rails—which she could see was necessary due to the height the contraption sat off the ground. The old man was covered with a blue plaid comforter. He looked better than she expected, and yet she noticed the blue-veined, thin hands gripping the blanket and the gaunt set of his cheeks.

"Mr. Hoffmaster," she said, walking closer. "Good to see you. I heard about your recent hospital stay."

The old man waved a hand at her and opened his mouth to speak. But phlegm caught in his throat, and he did that thing only old men know how to do with their throats to cough out the mucus. Nora reached for the tissue box, but he waved her off again while using a red-paisley handkerchief she hadn't noticed in his other hand to wipe away the gunk. The gesture and the handkerchief reminded her so much of her father, she had to look away, out the big bay window of the living room to the Hoffmaster's front lawn.

"Pardon me," Mr. Hoffmaster said, bringing her attention back to him. "Didn't mean to offend. Dang stuff just has a mind of its own these days." His voice sounded rough, raspy, but Nora could still hear the strength behind it.

"No, it's not that, I just ..."

He raised an eyebrow at her while blowing his nose, and this time, she waved him off.

"You didn't offend."

He gave a curt nod, finished wiping his nose, and laid his head back against the pillow as if spent from the action.

After a few seconds, he opened one eye without raising his head and said, "Have a seat."

She nodded and pulled a hard-backed chair that sat next to the bed closer. "Sarah said you guys wanted to get things in order."

He nodded and finally sat up. "I know your father and I had worked a few things out, but I couldn't find my paperwork and can't remember either." He reached out with his thin hand to tap her knee. "Don't get old, kid. It's the worst."

"You're not the first person to tell me." She offered him a wink and he chuckled. "But good news, I have a copy of your paperwork right here." She pulled the folder from her purse and tapped it with a finger.

Sarah walked back into the room and said, "Oh good. I'm so glad your father kept good records."

"Well, I wouldn't say *good*. You should have seen this file before I organized it."

Sarah laughed and looked at her grandfather. "Need anything, Gramps?" When he shook his head, she turned to Nora. "How about some tea or coffee?"

"Hot tea would be great if you have it. The weather is a little brisk today."

"Lemon?"

Nora shook her head, and Sarah walked into the kitchen. She noticed Sarah had grown a little thin too since the last time she had seen her. Caregiving and mothering would do that to a person. Perhaps she would talk to Dell about bringing them some food. Although she was not that great of a cook, she could whip up a casserole, and Natalie would probably offer to make something as well.

Mr. Hoffmaster laid his head back on his pillow and again closed his eyes, so Nora let the moments tick by without speaking, letting him rest. She could hear Sarah putting the kettle on the stove and pulling mugs from the cabinet. She checked to be sure she'd put her phone on silent and saw she'd missed a call from Gabe. She smiled and sent him a quick text.

NORA: With a client. Talk later?

A moment later his reply in the affirmative popped up, and she smiled. Should she feel bad about talking with another man while she was still engaged to Jake? Gabe didn't feel like a romantic man to her, just a friend. She'd loved chatting with him at the beach. Hearing how someone else didn't quite know what to do with their life had made her feel a little less alone.

A few minutes later, Sarah walked back into the room carrying another hard-backed chair. "It'll just take a minute for the water to boil. Should we start?"

Nora nodded as Sarah sat down next to her.

"Gramps? Are you able to stay awake for this, or should I just proceed on my own?"

Without opening his eyes or moving his head from the pillow, he said, "Proceed. I'll listen and let you know if you're screwing anything up."

Sarah laughed as she looked at Nora. "He's kidding. Mostly. Show me what you have."

"Well, your grandfather has picked out a casket—"

"A really nice one too, so don't change it."

Sarah smiled at his interruption but mouthed "Sorry" to Nora. She shrugged off the moment and continued.

"Here's a picture. Can you confirm, Mr. Hoffmaster? We wouldn't want to have the wrong one."

Nora held up the picture, and he squinted through one eye at it then nodded.

"And I assume you want to use Pastor Richfield for the service?"

At Sarah's nod, Nora checked off her note.

As they proceeded, Sarah agreed to what had already been determined and consulted her grandfather on the few things that remained. Just as they were starting to talk about what he might like for his obituary, the kettle squealed, and Sarah excused herself to the kitchen.

"How's your old man?"

The question startled Nora. Bud had been so quiet while she and Sarah consulted, she had thought perhaps he was asleep.

"Uh, he's fine. He's staying with Dell now."

Mr. Hoffmaster gave a snort. "Tough thing for a man to lose his house and his mind at the same time."

For a moment, Nora felt chastised, until the old man sat up and continued.

"Not that you and your brother had any choice, mind you." He squinted at her. "You ever been married?"

She shook her head, wishing Sarah would come back with the tea.

Mr. Hoffmaster raised his eyebrows and said, "Don't like men?"

"What? Oh no, I mean, yes. Uh ... I'm engaged to Jake Marshall." She didn't need to tell him she was thinking of calling off the relationship.

The man held her stare for a moment before plopping back onto the pillows. "You two been together a while now, I remember. What's the hold up?"

She swallowed hard as she tried to think of an answer. This was the issue of living in a small town—everybody knew your business.

"I'm holding Jake off until we see what Dad needs," she finally said. The statement wasn't totally false, just not entirely the truth. She fanned herself with the folder. Why did just thinking about Jake cause her to flush?

Mr. Hoffmaster lay so still she wondered if he'd heard.

"Your dad ever talk about his childhood?"

She swallowed hard again, trying to keep up with the leap in conversation topics. "Not really, sir."

"Bud."

"Excuse me?"

"People call me Bud."

"Well ... I know, but I'm technically here in a professional capacity, sir. My dad wouldn't want me to become too familiar."

"I was wondering how long you were going to take that 'sir' stuff, Gramps. Would be worse if you'd called him Byron, though," Sarah said as she carried in a tray filled with a pretty pink teapot and matching cups. She set the platter down on a low table next to the bed and proceeded to pour. "I'll let you do your own sugar if you don't mind," she said to Nora. "I think people have their own tastes."

Nora agreed and accepted a cup from Sarah with slow movements, not wanting to be her normally clumsy self and break the pretty china pieces.

"Don't worry. They've been in the family forever, but I'm down to these two cups," Sarah whispered. "It's hard to keep things this pretty when you have rambunctious little boys around. I only bring these out for the good guests." She winked at Nora, holding out the sugar bowl.

Nora picked out two cubes of sugar from the small bowl and plopped them in her cup.

"Always hated my name," Mr. Hoffmaster continued, oblivious to their side conversation. "Don't know what my mother was thinking with that one. All my siblings had good names—James, Bobby, Michael ... then me. *Byron.*" The old man shook his head and hacked up another bit of phlegm before continuing. "Anyway. Your dad and I used to raise quite a bit of cane back in the day."

Mr. Hoffmaster—Bud—was at least five years older than her father.

"How did you know my dad?" she asked, bringing the teacup to her nose. A hint of bitter orange filled her nostrils. She took a sip of the hot brew. *Ahh ... Earl Grey.*

"Age didn't matter much back then. I think your dad was in the same grade as my younger brother Bobby. But your dad was more grown up from the beginning. Liked to do grown up things."

"Now don't go disparaging her father, Gramps. He's not here to defend himself."

"Who said anything about dispar ... what did you call it?" He wiped his nose with the kerchief again and cleared his throat. "Anyway. He didn't ever tell you about that time we were caught running away?"

Nora almost choked on a sip of her tea. "Excuse me? Running away? From what?"

"Here. This town. Our families." Bud laid back on his pillow and looked up at the ceiling. "My old man wanted me to work in the factory, and your daddy didn't want to run that funeral business, thought he needed to find his own purpose in the world. So, we hitched it out of town. Had plans to hitch all the way to York state. Not sure what we thought we would do there, though. And we really should have started off south for the warmer weather. But anything sounded better than the plans laid out for us."

Her father hadn't wanted to run the family business? Had he been trying to find his purpose too? And he'd run away, just as she'd done last week to the beach? Maybe defiance was in their blood.

"What happened?" The old man's story had her on the edge of her seat now.

But Bud had nodded off once again. Nora fought the urge to shake him awake, remembering his doting granddaughter sat right next to her.

"Oh, well, that happens," Sarah whispered. "Maybe this has all been too much for him. Perhaps we can work on the obituary another time."

Nora felt conflicted. She really wanted to hear more about this father she never knew but didn't want to overstay her welcome. She was here in a professional capacity after all.

She finished her tea, gathered her things, and let Sarah walk her quietly to the door.

Outside, Sarah wrapped her arms around herself and said, "Thank you for coming. I wish the circumstances were better. We should really try to get together for lunch sometime, though. Since we moved back for Gramps, I've not made many friends."

Sarah and her family had moved into Mr. Hoffmaster's large home with her brood to take care of him last year. Sarah's mother had lived here years ago, but Sarah had grown up somewhere else—Nora wasn't sure where. Nora wasn't sure what had happened to Sarah's mother.

"Does your mother come to visit?"

Sarah looked pained for a moment, and Nora hoped she hadn't made a faux pas. Her mother was still alive, she hoped.

"She does. But not often. She never liked living in a small town, so she moved down south, near Charleston. She loves living there."

Another person who'd run away from this little burgh. Someone who had succeeded.

But she'd left her family behind, and now her father was dying. Why wasn't she here? Could Nora do the same—run away from loved ones who needed her?

"Hey, do you still take pictures?" Sarah asked, interrupting her thoughts. "Gramps said you used to have a camera strapped around your neck all the time."

Sarah's question caught Nora a little off guard. Nora's dad had bought her an EOS Kiss for her eighteenth birthday. She'd carried that thing around for years, shooting everything and convinced she would be a photographer someday. But now the camera sat in a box in her attic. She'd replaced the EOS with a newer Nikon a few years ago, but she took pictures only rarely, like last week while at the beach.

The scenery had been so different in the Outer Banks, the waves so inviting with the blue and white crests—she couldn't help but take tons of pics. She rarely felt the creative urge in Millsburgh anymore. Although she thought she could take some of the changing seasons—of the leaves making their magnificent change ... to death.

"I take some for fun, just for myself really," she finally answered Sarah.

Sarah nodded and shuffled her feet. "Ah, well ... I was wondering if you would take a few of our family before Gramps ... well, so we would have them, you know? We don't have many pictures of us together, and I regret we didn't take more before Grandma died." She looked back to the house as a shout came from one of the boys. "But if you're not into the idea, I guess I could do it myself. Maybe I could find a tripod ..."

Nora liked the idea immediately. And Sarah had enough on her plate. She could do this one small thing. Plus, the fall leaves would create some great photos right now. Maybe she could find some creative spark here amid the same-old-same-old.

"Tell you what, let me think about it," she said. "I want to be sure I can do something nice for you with what I have, though I'm no professional. I'll let you know in a few days ... do you think we have that much time?"

Sarah wrapped her arms around her waist and nodded. "He's been eating well, so the doctors say he could live a few more weeks."

"Good." Nora reached out and touched Sarah's arm. "I'll call you in a day or two and let you know my decision. Even if I decide not to, we still need to work on the obituary."

Sarah nodded. "Thank you. That sounds great." She reached out and hugged Nora, which felt odd since she was here for business. But Nora gave in and closed her eyes.

Sarah smelled like lavender and fresh soap. When Sarah pulled back, Nora felt an immediate absence.

"We'll talk soon," she told Sarah as she stepped to her car.

As she pulled away, she thought of her father again, his mysterious past, and about the idea of taking pictures for someone other than herself. The thought sparked the bit of creative juice she had long since buried beneath all the other *stuff* of adulthood. She turned her car in the direction of the photography shop in town.

Time to see what's new in the world of photography.

Chapter Six

The little bell above the door dinged as Nora entered Hayduk's Photography Studio. She'd worked for Sam Hayduk back in her early thirties. She'd loved helping people pick out cameras and accessories, but Sam hadn't been able to pay her much, so she'd moved on to a bank teller job.

As she moved through the rows of accessories, she felt a familiar tingle. Lenses, tripods, filters, and other accessories lined the tall wall before her. There were a lot of new things she hadn't seen before. She'd not been in this store in a long time.

"Well, look what the cat drug in."

She turned to see Sam, now a little bit grayer around the temples, limping toward her.

"Aren't you a sight for sore eyes. What's kept you away?" Sam pushed her shoulder with a playful tap.

"Hey Sam, life has kept me away. You know how it is."

"Uh, don't I ever. Let's go back here and sit down." He motioned for her to follow him behind the counter where two stools sat.

Nora remembered sitting here day after day flipping through camera catalogs and dreaming about being a big-shot photographer someday. Too bad being a photographer really didn't pay the bills.

"Why are you limping so? Did you hurt your leg?"

Her old boss tapped his hip with a finger. "Need a hip replacement. Too many years standing on my feet I guess."

"I'm sorry to hear that."

She guessed Sam to be in his early sixties. Still young in her eyes, but obviously time had worn down his body as it's known to do.

"Yep, I gotta set up the surgery, but I need to put things in order here first." He gazed around the store with a smile. "Gonna miss the place."

"Well, I'm sure it'll only be a few weeks, right? Maybe I could help out—"

"Oh no," Sam interrupted. "I guess you didn't hear. After my surgery, I'm moving to my daughter's over in Maple Grove. I'll be closing down the store unless I can find a buyer."

Nora felt a pang of loss. The store had been around for years, ever since Sam started it in his early twenties—right around the time she'd been born. He'd been a staple of the community, providing every imaginable photography need.

"That's too bad. I wish I could help." She really did. Wished she had whatever money he wanted to buy the place and make it her own.

Maybe I could get a loan ...

"How much are you asking for the place?"

"Well ..." Sam scratched the stubble on his chin. "Already talked with a lawyer about that. About $500,000."

Ugh.

She'd never have that much money, even with a loan ... if she'd qualify for one.

"That's too bad. I do truly wish I could help."

Sam waved her off. "Didn't mean to bring you down with my blues. What can I help you with?"

🍁 🍁 🍁 🍁 🍁

Nora returned home an hour later with a bag full of accessories, feeling invigorated and revived. Sam had been very helpful in helping her pick out a few accessories, like a tripod and different lenses.

She'd dropped a decent amount of money on the items, a chunk of change she didn't need to dish out right now, but she thought this might lead to something more. The expense was an investment. And listening to Sam talk about selling his business had given her an idea. She could take photographs like the ones she was going to do for Bud and his family. The business wouldn't take up much of her time, and she could still help at the funeral home. Plus, she wouldn't need the overhead Sam had since she wouldn't need a building or anything, just some props and a few more accessories once she had some more disposable cash.

She fiddled with her camera a bit, trying out different settings. She played with the video feature a bit and thought maybe she could offer some video options. She didn't know of any other photographers in Millsburgh offering family portraits.

She flipped through the photos she had recently taken. Sunsets, shells, and a few of Gabe's dog Daisy were all she had to remember her time in the Outer Banks. When had she stopped loving photography? She used to take photos of everything—landscapes, still life ... anything that interested her. But when she was in her twenties everything interested her. Life was an endless sea of possibilities.

She turned again to the photos from last week. They were well framed, at least to her eye. In the one, Daisy bounced along the shoreline. Nora had caught the pup just slightly in midair as the wave hit. Daisy looked like she was smiling.

She took a minute to text the photo to Gabe with the caption "Flight of Fancy." He quickly texted back "Aw! I love it. Thanks." She smiled at the newfound friendship before returning to her purchases.

She thought about Sarah's request to photograph her family and felt a bit of bubbly excitement. Despite the motive being for a sad reason, she loved the thought of capturing families' most cherished moments. Her mind started to run with ideas, about how to pose the family while not highlighting Mr. Hoffmaster's—Bud's—bed situation. She wondered if he could sit in a chair. Maybe Sarah had some special item she would want to include in the photos. Her grandmother had died a few years ago from cancer, but maybe she had a photo she could hold or a special item from her to include.

Nora grabbed a notepad and began to jot down her ideas. Before long, the sun had moved across the sky and the day had flitted away.

Chapter Seven

Dell walked into Nora's house the next morning, took out a coffee mug, poured himself some coffee, then sat down beside her where she had been reading over her camera's manual and eating some yogurt.

"Make yourself at home," she said.

Dell raised his eyebrows at her before taking a sip of coffee. Grimacing, he put the cup back down and rose to grab the sugar bowl. "Gees, what kind of tar is this? Who taught you to make coffee?"

"You did." She turned back to her manual as Dell grunted.

"You could never get the ratio right."

"A scoop of coffee for every cup of coffee, right?"

Dell looked at her with wide eyes. "No wonder it's so strong." He rose to pour the liquid out in the sink.

"I'm kidding!" she yelled before he could dump the brew. "It's just a dark roast. Sorry it's not your bland donut-shop brand."

Dell returned to the table, dumped three spoons of sugar into the brew, and stepped to the fridge to add some creamer too.

"What are you doing here?" she asked, pulling her own mug of java closer. "Didn't Natalie make coffee today?"

"She had a doctor's appointment with one of the kids, so she didn't have time to make any. I had to get the others ready. Ethan had a meltdown right before the bus came because he couldn't find his shoe. And Katie cried because Ethan cried." He took a sip of his coffee. He winced again but took another sip. "I finally got them all bundled off and took Katie to preschool. Figured your coffee would be made and free, unlike that new coffee shop in town that charges five dollars and puts a ton of other froofu stuff in it."

Nora laughed. "Sounds like you've had quite the morning." She frowned. "Where's Dad?"

"One of his aides is there this morning, which gives us a bit of time to do our own thing, and they work with him on his cognitive stuff."

"What's that cost?" Nora asked.

"I don't want to know." At her raised eyebrows, he said, "It's supposedly covered. For now." Dell sipped his brew then gave her his full attention. "Now that I have some liquid energy coursing through my bloodstream, I'm hungry." He stood to grab a container of cookies from the pantry.

Nora scowled. "I think you make yourself a bit too comfortable around here, brother. What if I were saving those Milanos for something special?"

Dell paused with one of the sandwich cookies to his mouth and raised an eyebrow. "Are you?"

Nora held her narrowed gaze at him a moment more and laughed. "No. If I did, they would never get eaten."

Dell held one of the cookies out to her, and she snatched it. "What's all this?" he asked, motioning to the camera and new accessories.

Nora stood to refill her coffee mug, topped off Dell's too, and snatched another cookie. "I had an idea after talking with Sarah and Bud yesterday."

"What idea?" Dell said before shoving a cookie in his mouth. Bits of the treat fell from his lips, and Nora handed him a napkin.

"Neanderthal. Don't speak with your mouth full." She waited until he had cleaned up the crumbs before continuing. "Sarah asked me to photograph her family before her grandfather dies. You know, something to remember his last days while he's still good enough to do it. I took some good pics at the beach too, and I could take some of the fall colors happening right now. Maybe the little coffee shop in town would hang some of my photos. Maybe even sell a few. I mean not of Sarah's family, just landscapes."

Dell nodded as he swallowed the cookie he was chewing. "I like it. And you were always good with the camera."

She nodded. "Thanks. I'm thinking of starting my own photography business. Did you know Sam is sell—"

"Hold up," Dell said, holding up his hand. "We have a business to run, little sister. Or did you forget?"

"Not *our* business. Dad's business." She poked his shoulder with her finger. "And now yours. I've never really been part of the funeral business."

"That's not true. I need you. I can't run the place by myself." Dell frowned.

"I'd still help. But I need to do something for myself, Dell. The funeral home business isn't my purpose."

"You think it's mine?" Dell raised his eyebrows.

"Yes," she said. "Dad took you under his wing and showed you the ropes long ago. He barely told me where the files were kept."

"He means for us to run the business together."

"Again, I *will* help you. But I need something of my own. Picking out caskets and urns for people is not my purpose."

Dell put the cookie container away and wiped his hands on her kitchen towel. "Have you touched base with Jake?"

He's really good at changing subjects.

"Yeah, but only briefly. He had to go out of town to Vermont for business so we're going to have dinner when he gets back."

"You didn't talk about calling off the wedding?"

She sighed. "No."

"Well, maybe you can take some time for Dad today instead?" Dell asked. "You could ask him about this new business idea."

She doubted Dad would even understand. "Of course. I haven't spent much time with him lately. It would be good to catch up with him."

Dell paced the kitchen floor. "Well, don't be upset if he doesn't ... you know..."

"Know me? Has he forgotten you yet? Have the signs gotten worse?"

Dell sat down at the table and picked up one of her new lenses. After he fiddled with the lens for a few minutes, Nora put her hand on his to still the nervous action. "Dell?"

He winced. "It's getting worse, for sure. He repeats himself a lot. Can't find the words for things. Feels overwhelmed easily." Dell paused, taking a deep breath. "While you were gone, we had some ... incidents."

"What kind of incidents?" Nora set the camera manual aside and gave Dell her full attention.

"He, uh, well ..."

"Out with it, big brother."

"He became overwhelmed one day and hit Natalie. Just a slight smack is all. But he took hold of Ethan on another day. The noise from Ethan's video games upset him."

Nora remembered the other day when their father had complained about her nephew's games.

"He *hit* them? Dell, what did you do?"

Her brother wiped his hand over his face. "Not much to do. The caregiver we hired has given us some ways to deescalate situations and redirect. 'Put on a new hat,' she calls it. Keep things simple. And we're trying to make sure he's not alone with the kids."

Nora shook her head. "What are we going to do? You guys can't deal with that. Maybe he should move in here. I could—"

Dell held up a hand to stop her. "Natalie and I have discussed this." His brow pinched as he hesitated. "We've put him on the waiting list at Ravensbridge LIFE Center."

Nora stood. "What? Without asking me? You know I don't want him in a home, Dell."

"You weren't here, Nora. And this is my family. He hit my wife and child! It's not going to get better, and I'm not equipped to deal with it."

Nora strode to the coffeepot and poured herself another cup of the dark liquid as her own blood boiled.

"Ravensbridge LIFE Center? What kind of name is that?"

Dell leaned back in his chair. "Ravensbridge is the company who bought the home from the small family who owned it previously, and LIFE stands for Living Independence for the Elderly. They have a memory care wing."

This was the one thing she'd not wanted to happen. Putting their father in a home felt so ... so selfish. Their dad had taken care of them, fixed their scrapes and broken toys, consoled them when friends fought them, and given advice when things in their lives had gone astray. And now they were just going to give up and put him away in a home?

"Dell, I can't. We need to try something else. He can move in here. I'll—"

"Nora, no." Her brother stood and put his hands on her shoulders. "I can't imagine what might happen with you and him here alone. What if he lashed out at you? How could you defend yourself? Or what would you do? And you want to start this new business. How will you do that if you're taking care of Dad?"

"We can hire someone full-time."

Again, Dell shook his head. "Do you know how much full-time care in the house costs? We can't do it. Insurance only covers so much."

"He's done so much for us, Dell."

"You don't think I know that? When Mom was dying ..." Dell ran a hand over his face again. "This is the best way we can help him, I promise. We can still go every day to see him and keep up with him, but we can also live our lives while knowing he's being well cared for. Ravensbridge is full of qualified people."

She moved to sit down at the table again, coffee mug held between her hands, which had suddenly turned cold. This wasn't the way, she was sure of it.

"How long is the waiting list?" Maybe she'd have time to convince her brother that they could do this. She'd visit more, learn from the aide.

"I don't know. His moving in depends on when people ... move out."

They knew all too well about that aspect of life. Death brought change for everyone. Nora tried not to think now about that day when her dad truly left them. Would they feel like they'd experienced two deaths?

"Listen," Dell said, bringing her back to the moment. "I'm sorry I didn't tell you sooner, and I'm sorry to put a damper on your new business idea, but I really need your support. Starting a new business is not a great idea right now." He put a hand on her shoulder. "Listen, I have to go. The aide is only at the house until ten today, and I have errands to run. I'm not sure when Natalie will be back."

Nora nodded and stood, putting on a brave face. "Take your time. I'll go down to the house and hang out with Dad when the aide leaves. You just do what you need to do." She hoped she sounded selfless, when really she just wanted time with the aide alone. Maybe she could figure out a way to keep Dad with them in the house. Maybe even see for herself how he was doing. Surely the moment with Natalie and Ethan had been an isolated incident.

Dell nodded, kissed her forehead, and headed for the door. "Thanks, Sis. Again, I'm sorry." He turned back at the door and wrinkled his brow. "I know this is for the best."

Nora watched Dell head to his car. This certainly was *not* for the best, and she would show him.

Chapter Eight

Nora entered Dell's house about ten minutes later. She found her dad and the aide at the kitchen table with some brightly colored cards in front of them.

"Hi," she said to the young woman sitting with her father. "I'm Nora. Dell's sister."

The aide looked up from their activity and greeted her. "Hello. Nice to meet you. My name's Claire. Your dad and I were just doing some exercises."

"Dumb exercises," her dad mumbled as he focused intently on the cards laid before him, showing cartoon-like pictures of various items.

Nora sat at the table with them. "Don't let me stop you. Can I watch and learn?"

"Is that okay, Ned?" Claire asked her father.

He grunted but didn't verbally reply, his focus intent on the cards before him.

"These are kind of a matching game," Claire told her.

"Kids' game," her father mumbled. He looked up at Nora and said, "I don't know why you kids can't do these things yourself."

The aide glanced at Nora, but said to Ned, "Can you tell me which one of these other cards goes with the snowflake."

Nora's father scowled but concentrated back on the cards. He stabbed his finger at the snowman.

"Yes! Exactly," Claire said in her cheerful voice. "I'm going to mix them up a bit now and you can start again, okay? In the meantime, I'm going to talk with your daughter in the other room."

Claire moved the cards around the table, mixing them from where Ned had matched them up. When she was done, she motioned for Nora to follow her to the living room where they could still see her father but talk without being heard.

"Although the matching cards are something we use with most clients, I don't want to keep irritating him with it. He obviously feels like it's a bit too 'dumbed down' for him. Do you have things your dad would relate to we could use in our exercises that might be more calming for him? Sometimes patients can connect to things they have interest in."

Nora thought for a moment. "What about fishing lures? Dad did some fishing on his off days. Or photos?"

Claire nodded. "The photos would be good. Although those sometimes bring up big emotions, and we don't want to upset him. But chatting about things they do remember helps. And maybe we could use the lures and ask him what each was used for?"

"Yes, I think that would work. I have to go across the street to his house to get them. Be right back."

Nora hustled across the street and into her father's garage using her key. Thankfully, both her and Dell had keys to access everything inside her father's house. She rummaged in her father's tackle box, looking at the vast array of lures, bobbers, and line. She'd never gone fishing with her dad— she couldn't remember why or if Dell had ever gone—so she wasn't sure what each thing really did or what she should take.

Overwhelmed, she shut the case and decided to bring the whole thing. She went next into the house and found two photo albums—one of herself as a child and one with Dell.

She carried each item back across the street to Dell's house and into the kitchen. She set the albums on the kitchen counter and placed the tacklebox in front of her dad.

"What's this?" he asked, sliding a hand over the box.

"Your tacklebox. I thought you could show us what each thing is used for."

Claire smiled. "That's a great idea, Nora. Ned, I'd love to know a little bit about fishing."

Nora's father opened the tacklebox and ran a hand over the top tray. "I used to have this all organized." He looked at Nora with a stern expression. "Did you mess with this? You know I've told you to leave my stuff alone. You could get hurt on one of these lures, Nora girl!"

Nora blinked hard, before sitting down at the table while Claire tried to calm her father.

"Ned, can you show me what this one is for?" She reached to touch one, but Nora's father swatted her hand away.

"Be careful! You'll cut yourself." He slammed the lid shut and snapped the locks. "Darn kids. Always getting into my stuff."

Nora felt helpless at his display of anger. She had only wanted to help.

Claire stood calmly and reached for the box. "We can just put this away for now." She pointed to the albums. "I think Nora also brought some photos with her. Didn't you, Nora?" She looked at her with a calm smile.

Nora stood quickly and grabbed the photo albums while Claire moved the tacklebox from her father's hands and into the living room.

"Dad, look at this. Do you remember that old oak in the front yard? And the swing." She laughed and pointed to a photo in the album. "Here you are pushing me on it. Remember?"

Her father's scowl softened as he looked where she pointed. He laughed. "You always were a tomboy, weren't you? Look at those scuffed up jeans."

"Well, I didn't want to get anything nice dirty. Mom would have killed me."

Her father turned the page and ran a finger over a picture of his wife. "Where is your mother? I haven't seen her today."

Claire came back from the living room and sat quietly, watching their interaction.

"She's, uh, gone."

Claire held up her hand so only Nora could see and shook her head, indicating she shouldn't say more about her mother's death.

Her father nodded as he flipped the page of the album. "Look! There's your grandmother holding you. I remember that day. She had come to visit just for the weekend when a snowstorm hit, and she had to stay for a week. Your mother was fit to be tied."

Nora nodded. "I vaguely remember that. Didn't Mom get lost in the snow or something?"

Her father laughed. "Yes! She got so sick of Grandma butting in and criticizing everything she did. She went for a walk but got turned around in the blizzard. She was pert near frozen when she returned an hour later."

Claire smiled at Nora as they continued reminiscing.

An hour later, Nora had put the albums away and helped her father to his room for a nap. She wished she could crawl into his bed with him. She'd felt like she'd stood on a knife's edge for the last hour, wondering what might set Dad off or cause a large wave of emotion she couldn't handle. And she hadn't even talked with him about the funeral home or her new business idea.

"Thank you for your suggestions," she said now to Claire. "Not only did looking at the albums help Dad, it helped me too. I really need to hold onto these memories." She opened the door and walked out onto the porch with Claire. "But what happened with the lures? I'm surprised he let that go so quickly. But the photos seemed to erase the anger."

Claire clutched her coat tighter around her waist. "We can never really be sure what triggers these things. But when a big emotion or outburst happens, removing the item and redirecting them is the best course of action. Sometimes just giving them a different hat to wear helps."

"A different hat? Dell mentioned this to me earlier." Nora frowned. "I don't understand."

"Your dad needed to put on a different hat ... he had to put himself in another situation, another moment in time. The photos helped him to forget the lure issue—whatever it was. By looking at the photos, he was put into another time, place, and emotion. Obviously, he was very concerned about you and your brother being hurt by the lures, and he retained that worry. But the photos offered good memories and emotions."

Nora nodded. "That's good to know."

"It can be easy to distract them, to tamp down the upsetting emotions, if we simply acknowledge their emotion then reposition them to a new thing."

"We don't want to really try to calm them down, just distract them?"

"Redirect is what we like to say. Pointing them in a new direction. Giving them a new hat."

Nora nodded again. "It's a lot to take in and learn. I feel the tension in my shoulders."

Claire pulled out a pamphlet from her bag. "That's why I'm here. And here's some literature that might help." She stepped down off the porch and strode to her car, promising to be back in two days.

Nora watched her drive away and felt a wave of fatigue wash over her. She'd been wrong to leave Dell to deal with this alone. This was too much for one person. And they'd not been trained but just learning as they went along while their father's disease progressed.

Maybe this wasn't the time to start a new business. But how could she find her purpose? Maybe her purpose was just taking care of Dad. Yet, she felt so exhausted after only one afternoon.

She walked back into the house and read quickly through the pamphlet. There was a list of things that can often help the patient wear the "new hat" or to keep them engaged in a good way as Claire mentioned. She noticed looking at photo albums and sharing memories was one. She flipped through the photo album again, pausing to feel her own emotions about each picture. She wondered what feeling emotions the way her father was now was like—in such a deep way that he couldn't disconnect from each one anymore.

She ran her finger down the picture of her mother just as her father had. Each of them had found their purpose in life—her father with the funeral home and her mother as a real estate agent. How could she find hers?

Chapter Nine

Nora met Jill for lunch at Peretti's that Thursday. Jill had already found a table and had ordered two glasses of red wine. She was perusing the menu as Nora sat down.

"Hey, sorry I'm late. I was spending some time with Dad."

"How is he?" Jill sipped her merlot.

"He's doing good. I've been helping a little each day with the aide."

Jill slid the other glass Nora's way. "Catch up."

"I'm beginning to think you might just want to get me drunk, Jill Kendall."

Her friend looked up from the menu with a mischievous grin. "Not drunk, but ... relaxed."

Nora picked up her own menu and started looking at the prices. She should have asked Jill to meet her at a less expensive place.

"My treat," Jill said as if reading her mind. "I owe you for that time you brought my hubby lunch anyway."

"I did that as a favor, not to be repaid. You were out of town, and the man needed to eat."

Jill scowled and put her nose back to the menu. "He knows how to get takeout. And I want to do it, so just be thankful."

Nora sighed. *Fine. I should get the most expensive thing just to irritate her.*

"I doubt you'll be able to eat a whole portion of lobster alfredo," said Jill. "So maybe go with something a *bit* cheaper." She looked over the top of the menu and smiled.

"How do you do that?" Nora asked.

"You forget I know you too well." Jill put down the menu and leaned across the table. "Everything okay?"

"Dell and I had some words about Dad the other day. I feel like I came right back into the fire, you know? A week away was not enough."

"I get it," her friend said. "But how was the house? Was your time away good?"

"Yes. I even met a really nice man. But his story reminded me I couldn't run away from my problems. So, despite wanting to run away forever, I came back." She frowned.

"You don't feel rested at all?"

Nora thought about her question for a minute before saying, "I did. But I came back here to the same ol' stuff, ya know?"

Jill nodded, returning to her menu. The waiter came and took their orders—Nora refrained from the lobster alfredo and opted for a chopped salad instead. When he'd walked away, Nora fussed with her linen napkin and her fork.

"Earth to Nora," Jill said as she sat across from her. "You look far away."

"Thinking about things ... possibilities."

Jill raised her eyebrows and smiled. "Oh, that sounds promising. Spill."

"First off, your house is amazing. Thank you again for letting me use it. I think we need to make going there a regular thing."

Jill nodded. "Can do. Let's make it happen." She took another sip of her merlot.

Nora finally sipped hers too and sighed as the smokey liquid went down her throat.

When Nora opened her eyes, Jill was all smiles. "Tell me all about this mystery man you met."

Nora shrugged. "No mystery. His name is Gabe. We're just friends."

Nora liked Gabe, but he had decided to settle down in OBX and she couldn't leave Millsburgh. How could a relationship happen? She felt content to just be friends anyway. Gabe was more like another older brother to her.

"What about your dad? How's he?" Jill asked.

"Dell claims Dad is getting worse. I worked with him and the aide the other day. Although he does seem a little more short-tempered, I think he's doing okay. Dell is concerned, though, and put him on a waiting list for some nursing home." She wrinkled her nose. "I hate that idea, so I'm trying to work with the aide to see how I can prevent taking that step. It's hard, but I can see how Dell wants to protect his family. I should have noticed the issues before I left. Not sure if I made things better or worse by getting away."

"But you needed time to think. Did you at least do that?"

Nora nodded as the waiter brought their food. She dug a fork into the salad, suddenly very hungry. "I did, but things have changed in just that short time. The only thing I know for sure is I don't want to marry Jake. But I might have an idea about a new business."

Jill waved her own fork around with a bit of chicken parmesan on the end. "Other than the funeral home?"

Nora pushed the bits of her salad around the plate. Why didn't anyone understand the funeral home wasn't *her* thing?

"The funeral home is the boy's thing, not mine. I need something to call my own. To find my purpose."

"You must have been to church this week. Pastor Richfield's sermon get to you, huh?" Jill smiled.

Nora shrugged. "I've been trying to find my purpose ... my *thing* for a while now. The funeral home is not it. Just like the bank wasn't and the cashier job wasn't ... I've spent too many years trying to find my place in this world."

"Maybe you just need a bit of *zhush* at the funeral home to make the place your own. Put some new paint on the wall, bring in some flowers ... something you like."

Nora shook her head. "It's more than that. My dad is everywhere there. The filing is all in his handwriting, little notes he's made throughout the years. The desk is full of his photographs. I can even still smell the cigarettes he used to smoke. But it's more ... personal. He knew everyone and their families. Bud Hoffmaster even asked me about him the other day. The business won't ever be *just mine*."

Her friend nodded and took another bite of her meal. When she swallowed, she said, "I get it. What's your idea?"

Nora smiled and leaned in. "A photography business. Did you know Sam is selling the photography store?"

"I had heard rumors. Are you going to buy his place?"

Nora scoffed. "I wish. I can't afford to, unfortunately. I'm thinking of just taking family photos, you know, setting up props and whatnot."

"Won't you need a place to do that?"

Nora had considered this but wondered if she could just take them at the people's homes like she was doing for the Hoffmasters. "I don't think so ... not right now anyway."

"Starting a business is hard," Jill said. "When my family started their pretzel business, they were the only game in town, but now? There are a ton of competitors. Who else offers the same thing in this area?"

"I don't think anyone. That I know of anyway."

In truth, Nora didn't really know. Maybe someone *was* already offering this kind of thing.

"That would be my first step, I think," Jill said. "Check out the competition. See if the market is saturated already. Or figure out something special you could offer."

"I agree. Thanks. I'll consider that."

She noticed Jill stiffen as she heard the tinkle of the bell on the restaurant door. She turned to see Jake walking into the restaurant and to the front counter. He said something to the waitress and looked at their table. When his eyes met Nora's, he strode toward them with a wide smile.

"Hey, babe! Fancy seeing you here." He glanced at Nora's table companion. "Jill."

"Jake." Jill looked at Nora with wide eyes. When Nora gave a slight shake of her head, Jill took a huge gulp of her wine, then motioned to the waiter for more.

Nora turned to look up at Jake.

"I thought you were in Vermont," she said.

"Just got back. I texted you earlier about setting that dinner up, but you didn't text back."

"I-I ... I've been busy with my dad today and now lunch, so ..."

"I get it." Jake smiled, and Nora had to turn away.

Just because he's good looking doesn't mean you should marry him.

Jake leaned closer and put his hand on the back of Nora's chair. He whispered in her ear, "I really missed you. We should go away by ourselves soon."

She wanted to agree and just ... settle. Meeting men was so hard. Why couldn't she just love and commit to this one? But she knew their relationship wasn't right.

She leaned away from him and said, "I really need to stay here right now. Dell and I are dealing with some things with Dad."

He leaned in and kissed her cheek. "I understand. Dinner tomorrow?"

She sighed. He was relentless, but she needed to call the whole thing off and a public place would be ideal. *Would it?* She wasn't sure anymore. She had been so caught up in thinking about her new business idea and helping with Dad, she'd almost completely forgotten about Jake.

"Sure. Six?" She took another sip of her wine.

"Sounds good." He kissed her temple, nodded at Jill and headed back to the counter. The waitress held up a bag of food, which he snatched from her and tromped to the front door.

"Are you okay?" Jill asked, placing her hand over Nora's.

Nora held up her now empty glass. "I need more wine."

"You don't want to talk about how you just blew off your fiancé? You didn't even answer his texts? Nora, I know you want to end it, but he still deserves to be treated with respect."

"I know. I just need to plan out what I want to say. I fumble with my words around him right now, knowing I'm going to end the relationship but trying to play the loving fiancée. I was never good at being fake."

"But you will have a plan soon, right? You can't keep stringing him along."

Jill raised her eyebrows and Nora nodded. "Yes. At dinner tomorrow. But to be clear, he hasn't been all sunshine and roses. I'm not the bad guy here."

"I didn't say you were." Jill leaned in and wiggled her eyebrows. "Do you plan to make a huge display of the breakup? Throw your napkin or something?"

Nora thought about the idea for a moment, but let it pass. Jill was dramatic sometimes. "Not every interaction has to be so sensational, like in your novels. I'm not trying to sell a book here."

Jill affected a solemn gaze and put her hand to her heart. "I write academic books, Nor. There is no drama."

"I'm your friend, remember? I know you also secretly write juicy romance novels under a pseudonym. Those are the books I meant."

Jill smiled over the lip of her glass. "You can prove nothing. Until my death, anyway, when you better get those journals out of my house before Bob reads them."

When the waiter had refilled their glasses, her friend leaned toward her again and said, "How did you leave things with Gabe?"

"Friends. If that. We've texted back and forth a bit since I've come home, but he's dealing with his friend's death and starting his own new business with the widow."

"Grief upon grief." Jill shook her head. "But at least he has a fresh start with a new business, right? Maybe that's what you need."

"Maybe." Nora buttered a roll. "In any event, thanks for the use of your house."

Jill waved a hand at her. "No problem. I wish we could get down there more often. But I'm glad someone could use it. Tell me more about your business idea."

Nora proceeded to tell her about photographing Mr. Hoffmaster's family.

"That sounds like this opportunity might be good for you," Jill said as she scooped the last of her marinara with a roll. "I think you have a gift for photography, but you never seem to believe me. Maybe God has a purpose for that gift."

Jill had always commented on her composition when taking photos. And Nora was looking forward to taking the photos for the Hoffmasters. Could she somehow maneuver her love for photography into something that paid?

"How does Dell feel about this?" Jill asked.

Nora sighed. "He was not too impressed. Says he needs me at the funeral home."

"Couldn't you do both?"

"I think so. But you just said starting a business is hard work. I'll need to devote a lot of time to getting set up. And helping with Dad too."

Jill pointed her fork at her. "You need to talk to Dell. Tell him how you feel."

"I know. We just never dreamed Dad wouldn't be able to fulfill his duties or even care enough to ask questions about it. I think Dell might feel like I'm trying to abandon ship." Nora took a sip of her wine and swallowed.

"Are you?"

"No, not really. I still fully intend to help him." Although Nora knew in her mind she'd probably cut back more and more at the funeral home once her business took off.

"Can you ask someone else for help?" Jill sat back in her chair.

Nora had thought of that but wondered if the funeral home was making enough to pay someone—even part time.

"I guess Dell and I need to talk."

Jill nodded. "Sounds right." She picked up the small table card and looked at the dessert menu. "Let's split a tiramisu. Dessert solves a lot of things."

Chapter Ten

Nora stood outside the Indian restaurant—Indie Yum—worrying the cuticle on her thumb with her pointer finger while waiting for Jake to arrive. Not for the first time, she wondered what idea Jake had and how she'd finally break things off. The idea must be something big since he'd agreed to come to a restaurant he didn't like. Maybe she would just end things quickly before he had a chance to tell her about his idea. Maybe he wouldn't want to tell her his idea once she'd said what she needed to say.

She looked down at her outfit. She'd taken way too long to decide on what to wear for tonight. Especially for someone she believed wasn't right for her. Nora had settled on jeans that made her butt look smaller and a loose-fitted blue shirt with quarter-length sleeves despite wanting to be more carefree with her style. She already regretted not bringing a jacket or a cardigan. The slowly cooling night air blew right through her blouse. She clutched her Coach bag and shivered.

She checked the time on her phone again. She was early, but only by a few minutes. Once again, the differences between her and Jake appeared highlighted as if written in neon across the sky. Nora always liked to be early, while Jake had always arrived anywhere they went with just a few minutes to spare.

"I'm not late," he'd say. "I have two minutes to spare."

But to her, two minutes to spare was late. Her dad had always told her, "Early is on time, on time is late, and late is *unacceptable*." And she had adopted this philosophy for her own life.

But is that a reason to not marry someone?

She told her brain to be quiet.

What if he doesn't show?

That will just cement the deal. And I'll have dinner on my own.

Nora craned her neck to look down the block, hoping to see Jake's loping stride. *Hoping or dreading?* Instead, she saw Sarah Anderson walking with a man who was not her husband. Nora's eyes widened as Sarah laughed and grabbed the man's arm. They were walking right toward Nora, and she felt a moment of panic.

I can't let them see me! Or let them know I saw them. I don't need to be swept up into extramarital situations. She turned to head into the restaurant to wait for Jake, but Sarah's voice stopped her.

"Nora? Hey, funny seeing you here."

Nora turned with a wide, fake smile. "Hey, Sarah. How are you? How's your grandfather?"

Where is your husband? she wanted to ask but didn't. When had she become so judgmental? The question would be rude, of course, and the situation was none of her business. She looked at the man standing beside Sarah. Handsome, well built ... but so was Sarah's husband, Brian. Nora wondered briefly how long the affair had been going on

66

and how she thought she could get away with it by parading her boy toy around downtown for everyone to see.

"He's doing well," Sarah said. "So good, in fact, Brian said I should get out of the house and treat myself to a nice dinner."

A nice dinner, indeed. The nerve.

"Well, how nice." Nora turned to the man smiling down at her from Sarah's elbow. She offered her best scowl when she said, "And you are?"

The look on Sarah's face said it all. She removed her arm from the crook of the man's elbow and laughed.

Wait. Why is she laughing?

"Nora, this is my brother Luke. He came to visit when he heard Gramps wasn't well. He arrived after you left the other day."

"Oh! Oh ... ha." Nora held out her hand to shake. "Nice to meet you." She felt a flush of warmth enter her cheeks. How could she have thought Sarah would cheat on Brian and their three kids?

Luke offered a shy smile, his eyes never leaving Nora's, as he shook her hand in greeting.

"The funeral home lady, right?"

Drat. That's not attractive at all. He's probably envisioning me applying makeup to some poor old dead woman. Wait, why do I care if he finds me attractive?

Nora glanced down the street again, wondering what was keeping Jake.

"Yep, that's me." She removed her hand from Luke's and touched her throat. *Had it suddenly gotten warm?* She had been cold just a minute ago. She was not sure if she felt embarrassment or some kind of attraction. He *was* quite handsome. "But don't let that deter you. I do talk to live people sometimes."

What in the world? Where had that come from?

But Luke's hearty laugh made her smile as she felt a flush go to her cheeks once more.

"Are you waiting on someone?" Sarah asked. "We were just going into Indie Yum for dinner. Brian is taking care of the kids so my brother and I could catch up. Besides, I needed something besides chicken nuggys and mac and cheese."

The other woman laughed, and Nora could see she did truly need a night away. The dark circles under her eyes had been expertly covered with makeup, but Nora could still see the tiredness in her eyes. And not only from her kids but from the constant thoughts about her ailing grandfather.

"I ... I'm waiting for someone." Nora looked again at Luke.

Dark-haired and blue-eyed like Jake, she couldn't help but start making comparisons. For one, he was attentive to his sister and to her—someone he had just met. Jake would have been chattering about himself nonstop. And Luke had an air of ... what was it? Nora looked at his freshly pressed slacks with a sharp front pleat and what looked to be a matching, tailored button-down shirt. Not in the matchy-matchy or easy color kind of way—dark tan slacks with a sage green shirt. Maybe he was gay.

She brushed the thought aside as she heard her name called once more. She looked up to see Jake striding toward their little group. She barely recognized him in the black jeans and button-down white shirt with black blazer he was wearing.

Where did he get those clothes? She couldn't remember him even owning a blazer.

"Whew, I'm glad I caught you." Jake bent over and put his hands on his knees, trying to catch his breath. When he straightened, he said, "I know you hate when people are late."

She checked her cell phone's clock. *Yup, directly on time. Which meant late in her book.*

"You *are* late," she told him.

"We said six, right." He consulted his own cell's clock, then showed the screen to her. "Boom! On the dot."

She fought the urge to rub her temple to ward off the headache brewing behind her right eye. Why had she agreed to this? But he did look good, and she momentarily forgot about the couple standing next to her.

"Where are my manners. Jake, this is Sarah Anderson, Bud Hoffmaster's granddaughter, and her brother Luke."

Jake held out his hand to Luke first then Sarah. Nora didn't miss the subtle glance Luke offered her.

"Nice to meet you both. I know your grandfather, Sarah. How's he doing?"

Again, Sarah's pained look caused Nora's heart to constrict. She knew the pain of answering a question like that over and over again. But Nora could give Jake some credit. At least he had the sense to be cordial and caring in most situations. He had spent some time as a hospital volunteer during high school when he needed some extracurricular stuff for his college applications. Not that he had needed a college degree, since his father owned the largest manufacturing business in the area and planned to hand everything over to Jake at some point.

"He's hanging in there." Sarah bit her lip, looking away. Luke placed his hand on the small of her back and pulled her slightly closer to himself.

Nora's heart surged. This was how a man should treat a woman, even if Sarah was his sister.

"Hey, why don't you guys join us?" Sarah said, eager eyes looking at Nora.

Was the offer legitimate—someone trying to make a new friend—or did Sarah sense Nora's agitation and want to give her an out? Nora was sure everyone in town had heard about her and Jake's on-again, off-again relationship. Perhaps sitting together would erase the awkwardness she felt at being with Jake now. And they could avoid talking about their relationship. Although, she did really need to talk to Jake about calling off the wedding.

"Yeah! That would be great," Nora said, grinning. "The more the merrier, right?"

One more day couldn't hurt.

Jake jumped in. "This is your night out, Sarah. I'm sure you would prefer to just talk with your brother. Maybe some other time." Jake touched Nora's elbow and pinched.

Nora shook him off. "She made the suggestion, Jake."

"No." Sarah grabbed at Nora's arm. "Really. I'd like to get to know you better. And I could use more company to kind of forget what's happening at home. Please?"

Nora could have never refused after that—not that she wanted to—nor could she ever refuse the pained look in Sarah's eyes. She turned to Jake. "I know you wanted to talk about something, but let's just forget about all that tonight, okay?"

Jake shrugged. "It's cool. We can still chat with company."

Drat.

For a moment, Nora thought better of the decision. Maybe she should just let Jake say what he needed to say right out here on the street and have dinner by herself. Was this Jake's way of winning her over—dressing nicely and being courteous to others? He was sure to have suspected something despite her not being open and honest with him.

As Jake steered her forward into the restaurant, she felt a shift in the earth's normal pull.

Maybe having Luke and Sarah along would be best. She was glad he had suggested a public place—in case Jake said something that would cause her to want to flee again.

Chapter Eleven

"So, I said to this jerk hogging the fifty-pound weights, 'Hey man, stop making us wait for the weights!' Get it? I used the word wait two different ways." Jake slapped his hand onto the table making the silverware and dishes dance and guffawed.

Nora was glad Sarah had invited herself and Luke to dine with them—if only to keep her from listening to Jake's tired old stories by herself. She used to enjoy his boisterous, fun nature, but lately he seemed childish.

You can put the boy in different clothes, but it doesn't make a man.

Her father had told her that many times about Jake. He'd never been a fan of their relationship. Maybe that was why she couldn't commit. She needed her father's approval. And now she'd probably never get it. He barely remembered who she was—who knew if he remembered Jake.

She brought her attention back to the table. As Jake droned on, she wished he would let someone else talk. Especially Luke. She wanted to know more about him. He had deferred to Sarah on everything, including her favorite dish to order. He'd held her and Nora's chair for them prior to sitting himself while Jake had just flopped down and threw his napkin over his lap.

Now Luke and Sarah looked at each other and smiled. Jake's stories were starting to wear on them too. She had to jump in and save this night.

Nora cleared her throat. "So, Sarah, where do you and Luke originally hail from?"

Sarah ate the last of her food from her plate, then wiped her mouth with a napkin. "I'm a Jersey girl." She laughed, and Nora smiled back. "Mom moved there right before Luke was born."

"Illegitimate child, don't you know." Luke winked.

Sarah looked at her brother and smiled. "But thankfully, my mom met someone and got married soon after moving to New Jersey—my dad. We only visited Millsburgh a few times while growing up. Mom and Gramps didn't always get along." Sarah brushed a bit of crumb from the table, and Nora could sense her reluctance to share all the details of her family's dark corners. "But I loved the quiet here, and when Gram died, I knew Gramps would need someone to help out around the place." Sarah used her napkin to wipe the corner of her eye this time.

"And he's all the better because of it," Luke told her with a smile.

She nodded. "I hope so, but my family is happy here too. Although I do miss being closer to the beach."

"I would love to live closer to the beach," Nora admitted. "I was just in the Outer Banks for a week. The beach is so peaceful there."

"How did you afford that?" Jake horned into their conversation.

Nora had almost forgotten he was there, being so caught up in Sarah's story. She noticed he now had a smear of red across his chin. She fought the urge to wipe the sauce off for him.

"Jill let me use their beach house," she said instead, turning her attention back to her own barely touched meal.

Jake raised his eyebrows and stared at her for a moment. She pretended not to notice and poked at a few pieces of food on her plate. Nora hated the awkwardness for Sarah and Luke, but she didn't want him to have any claim over her life anymore. She turned her attention back to Luke and Sarah.

"My friend has a house there. It's not right on the beach, but close. She was very generous to let me stay there. I needed to get away for a bit."

"Yes, I heard about your dad," Sarah said. "Gramps talks about him now and again like he did that day you visited. The disease is so heart wrenching, I think. Never knowing if your loved one will remember you or—oh, I'm so sorry." Sarah brought a hand up to her lips. "That was completely insensitive of me."

Nora shrugged. "It's not untrue. And Dell and I are learning to live in the moment with Dad and appreciate any time he does remember." She didn't want to get into the fact that they might be moving Dad into a memory care facility.

Sarah nodded, reaching over to pat Nora's hand.

Jake chimed in again. "It's going to get hard."

Nora, wanting desperately to shift the conversation, turned to Luke. "What do you do for a living?"

Luke leaned onto his forearms. "I own a publishing company in Philadelphia."

"Oh, what kind of books does your company publish?" Nora loved books and read voraciously when she could find the time.

"Mostly nonfiction. Memoirs, coffee table books, art anthologies ... we have a very niche market. A lot of our works focus on photography first, with a story added in."

Photography. How ... coincidental.

"I've just started taking up photography again, so I would probably love your books."

Luke smiled as Sarah reached across the table again to grip Nora's hand. "You decided, yes?"

Nora nodded. "Your request really got me excited to start my photography again. I went downtown immediately after talking with you and bought some new accessories for my camera. Nothing fancy, but it'll get me started."

"Wait, what request?" Jake stopped scraping the last bits of food from his plate and turned to stare at her, eyes narrowed.

"Sarah asked me to take some professional photos of her family before—" Nora glanced at Sarah before continuing. "You know. *Before.*"

"But I thought you had given up photography?"

Jake's scrutiny boiled her blood. *What did he care?*

"People rarely give up something they love."

Sarah, Jake, and Nora turned to look at Luke.

"Well, I'm just saying. I could see in your eyes that you obviously love photography. You practically lit up the room when you just told Sarah yes."

The waiter came with their checks. Luke took both and said, "My treat."

Nora noticed Jake didn't try to argue, but she did. "No, Luke, let me get that." She reached for her purse but felt instantly angered at Jake and his lack of responsibility. He had invited her after all.

"Put your purse away. I got this. You can get the next time." Luke winked, pulled out his black card, put it with the check, and looked at his sister. "Sarah told me she had asked you about photographing Gramps, and I think it's a great idea. You could give us a discount since I paid for dinner." He smiled at Nora, and she felt her heart melt just a little.

"I'll give that some thought." She smiled back. "I think it's a great idea too, and I'm glad Sarah mentioned it. In fact, I think I might like to start my own photography business—taking family portraits. Maybe senior pictures or engagement photos." Nora couldn't contain her smile.

Luke leaned forward over his dinner plate and gave Nora his complete attention. "What kind of accessories did you get?"

Nora mirrored his position, leaning over her own now empty plate. "The salesman suggested a few different filters and a cool new tripod. I can't wait—"

"Wait, wait, wait." Jake waved a hand between her and Luke. "You want to start another business? What about the funeral home?"

Nora turned to Jake. "I'll still work there, but part-time once my business takes off." When she saw the look on Jake's face, she added, "Is there an issue?"

Jake opened his mouth to say something, but then closed it again. Finally, he said, "No problem. Sorry. This just took me off guard. I ... I thought you wanted to get out of Millsburgh."

"Well ... I did at one point, but I can't leave now with Dad the way he is. Dell does need me for both the home and Dad."

"I-I just, um ..." He looked at Sarah and Luke and back to Nora. "Can we talk privately?"

"Oh, we can leave as soon as we get Luke's card back," Sarah chimed in. "We're sorry. We shouldn't have—"

Nora held up a hand. "No need to apologize. I enjoyed our dinner." She smiled at Luke, then turned back to Jake. "How about we chat tomorrow?"

"I really need to talk to you tonight, today ... now."

The waiter came back with Luke's card and the siblings stood to leave.

"It was really nice to meet both of you," said Luke. "I'm looking forward to chatting more some other time."

With a wave from Sarah, they headed out of the restaurant.

Nora turned back to Jake. "Okay. The floor is yours."

Jake smiled and took her hand. "I have been waiting to tell you and just finished up all the arrangements while I was Vermont."

"What arrangements?"

"I bought us a house! You'll love it. It's right on a lake and there is—"

She threw down her napkin. "You bought *us* a house? In *Vermont*? What are you talking about?"

"My uncle runs part of my dad's business up there. He's older than my dad by about six years, and he wants to retire. We decided I would take over up there when he retires." He smiled again. "I wanted this to be a surprise. You always talk about moving away from here. When you went to the beach, I knew this could be a way for us to get away from here. To start a new life together."

Nora couldn't believe what she was hearing. "But you didn't ... you never considered talking with me first about this? You just ... did it? My dad is ill, Jake. I have to help Dell, to help run the business. I can't just move hundreds of miles away."

Nora stood from the table, grabbed her bag, and began to walk away. Jake called to her, and she held up her hand to shush him. "Jake, I came here tonight to end our relationship.

I thought doing so would be hard, but you've made breaking things off so easy. I can't move. And I don't want someone who doesn't consult me in major decisions. We're done."

She pushed her own thoughts from her mind as she strode from the restaurant. Nearing her car, she pulled her keys out of her purse and pressed the door lock button. The blip of the doors unlocking was followed by Jake calling her name.

"Nora, wait! We have to talk about this."

She glanced back to see Jake loping quickly across the parking lot toward her. She quickly got in the car, turned on the ignition, threw it into drive, and pulled away.

Chapter Twelve

Nora returned home and stomped into her house. *What was he thinking? Does he not see how messed up this is?* She paced the living room while texting Jill about the moment. As Jill's text came back, Nora heard a car pulling into her driveway. She looked out the front window and saw Jake's car skid to a stop in the early gloom of the evening.

She walked out onto the porch gripping her waist. The air had suddenly grown colder, and Nora chastised herself for not grabbing a sweater ... again. She could grab one from inside, but she wanted to keep Jake out.

Jake took his time getting out of his Ford Mustang, acting as though he had to organize the entire interior before exiting. Finally, he swung open the door and got out, throwing his sunglasses back onto the dashboard.

As he approached, she asked, "Why are you here?"

Jake put up his hands in surrender. "We can't just end things the way you did at the restaurant."

She remained silent as he walked up to the porch.

"Can we go in?" Jake asked, moving toward the door.

She held out her hand to stop him. "No. We can make things simple, Jake. We're done."

Jake smoothed his hands over the front of his jeans and looked down at his sneakers. "Can we at least sit?"

Nora relented, dropping her defensive stance, and moving to the two rocking chairs. There was no way she was sharing a seat on the swing with him.

Both of them at one time or another had "ended" the relationship. Their relationship had more ups and downs than the Appalachian Trail. And she wasn't really angry, just done. She didn't have time for any more emotional trauma.

She needed to move on with her life. Her dad and her family needed her now. She needed to find her own path, her own purpose. Maybe she would never be married, but she would always have Dell, Natalie, and the kids.

Jake plopped down onto the chair next to hers and proceeded to rock. "Man, I love this porch. Remember when we used to sit out here on the swing"—he looked at her with a smile—"and just chat for hours?"

Nora remained silent as she rocked, silently praying whatever this was would end quickly so they could both move on. She wrapped her arms around her middle again, longing for a jacket.

When she didn't reply, Jake sighed and said, "You ran off so heated and ... and well, I didn't want to leave things that way. I don't know why you got so upset."

Again, she remained silent, eyes fixed on the bumper of his ridiculous car.

Jake wiped his hands on his jeans again. "Okay, so you're mad at me. I can handle that. You've been mad before."

She sighed. "How could you just go and decide something without checking with me first?"

"You mean like going away for a week without telling me or deciding to start your own business without discussing it?"

Nora winced. He had her there. "You're right. I think it's pretty obvious neither of us is truly in this relationship. Not in the right way anyway. We've tried for years. But we're too different, too stubborn, too—"

Jake held up his hand and she stopped. "I agree."

He ... *agreed*?

Before she could say more, he continued, "I didn't agree until tonight. I saw the look in your eyes when you started talking about the photography. I'm not blind. But I had wanted to work on us, make us better. When you went to the beach, and this Vermont idea came up, I just ran with it, thinking you'd be so happy with me when you came back. And we could finally start our real life together."

She held up her hand this time. "My dad is ill, Jake. I have a business here to run. Family here who need me. I can't just move hundreds of miles away. What made you think I could?"

Jake nodded. "I see what you see now. I sometimes just get carried away, wanting to make others happy. I really, truly, was trying to make you happy, I swear. You always talk about moving away from here. I thought I was doing something for us."

Nora opened her mouth to respond but couldn't come up with a single thing to say.

"Anyway, I just wanted to let you know I'm still taking the job in Vermont. I'll be moving at the end of this month."

"What?" She frowned. "You're still moving?" She didn't know what to think of this information. Everything had been turned upside down so quickly.

Jake nodded. "Yep. My uncle is already planning his retirement. I can't let him down, and there's nothing keeping me here now."

Nora sat in stunned silence.

Jake sat back against the rocker and wiped a hand over his face. "I ... I really regret how things always were with us and ... well, I thought getting married and moving away from here would fix everything, but I see now it won't. And besides, we just don't really work, do we?" Nora offered him a withering smile.

"I tried, Nor, I really did."

"We had a lot of issues. More than a magazine subscription."

He laughed. "When you left the other week, I had a moment of panic that I would never see you again." He glanced at her, but she remained silent. "I was so happy to see you again and wanted to make things better. But this wasn't the way for you. I see that now."

Nora stood and moved toward the steps. "I'm happy for you and wish you all the best."

Jake followed her down into the yard, kicking a bunch of grass with his shoe. "I really didn't want to go to Vermont by myself. I truly thought we could do this together. I'm sorry."

"No need to be sorry now. We're finally on the same page. My place is here. I have my family and my own ... gifts to focus on." She paused, considering for a moment what all this recent talk about gifts truly meant. "Have a great life, Jake."

Jake opened his mouth to say more but snapped his lips shut before saying anything. When he reached out his hand, she took it, and he pulled her close. His lips brushed her temple, and she closed her eyes as he pulled her in for a hug. She felt sad. Not for the relationship that didn't work, but for the time they'd wasted trying to be something they weren't.

Jake stepped back and looked at Nora with mournful eyes for one more moment, then turned, got into his car, and drove away.

Chapter Thirteen

Nora was at Dell's front door a few minutes later, wanting some comfort and to tell him she and Jake were through. She tried the front doorknob, but found it locked, so she knocked. She should have brought her key.

A moment later, the door opened slowly, and she looked down into her nephew Mason's eyes. From somewhere in the house, she could hear the adults yelling.

"What's going on, buddy?"

Mason said nothing but opened the door wider.

The other three kids sat sullenly on the couch listening to the shouting match coming from the other room. Nora moved swiftly inside to sit between them and drew them to herself.

"What's going on?"

Mason refused to be drawn into her hug while the other three cuddled close. "Pop Pop is angry at Mom for cooking peas."

"That's not it, stupid," Ethan said, a scowl looking unnatural on this little face. "It's his crazy mind, that's all."

"We don't say crazy, E," Nora reminded him. "Pop Pop just has some lapses in memory, remember? And we don't call people names."

"He's scary. I don't like him anymore." Little Katie huddled closest to Nora, trying to burrow herself under her aunt's armpit.

Nora shushed her and kissed the top of her head. "It's okay. Is your dad here?"

She heard Dell's shout, a door slam, followed by the sound of crying. *Natalie*. Nora could hear Dell's hushed voice trying to soothe her. Soon, another door clicked shut, and Dell was standing in front of them.

"Nor? I didn't hear you come in." Her brother shoved his hands through his hair, and Nora noticed the dark circles under his eyes and a scruff of a beard as if he hadn't shaved in a few days. He looked like life had run over him with a bulldozer. Then she noticed a red mark on the left side of his face.

"Are you okay?" she asked, still holding the kids tight. All except Mason who had run to his dad's side and grabbed his hand.

"Yeah." Dell looked down at his oldest son. "Hey, buddy. Everything okay out here?"

"Katie won't stop crying, and Ethan is being annoying."

"Am not! I just wanted to play my video game."

"But I told you to sit still and—"

"STOP." The boys fell quiet at Dell's raised voice. "Please go back to your rooms for a bit. Mommy will be making dinner soon."

Mason stomped off to his room while Ethan took Katie's and Brett's hand and led them away. Katie sniffled as she passed Dell, and he stopped the trio long enough to wipe her tears and kiss them each on the cheek. "Everything will be okay. I know this was scary, but everything is fine now. Go to your rooms and shut the door. I'll come get you shortly."

The three nodded as Ethan pulled them gingerly toward the stairway. Nora could hear their little feet padding up each step and the click of their doors.

Dell plopped onto the couch next to her.

"What in the world was that?" she asked.

Dell sighed. "Dad. I told you. He gets these ... he gets upset sometimes."

"Are you okay?"

Dell put his head in his hands and bent over at the waist. "No," was his muffled reply.

Nora rubbed her brother's back and let him decompress from the tense moment. She wondered if there was more she should do but was unsure of what. She should have moved Dad into her home. Or moved in with him in his own. When Dell didn't respond further, she pushed herself off the couch and went to her father's bedroom door.

She entered with a light tap so he would know she came in peace. Her father sat on his bed, elbows on his knees, looking as if a dark cloud had descended on his life.

"When's dinner?" he asked her.

Or maybe he's just hungry.

She stepped tentatively into the room. Dell hadn't said what had set their father off—it couldn't have really been peas—and she didn't want a repeat of the shouting she had heard a moment ago. Faintly she heard someone, probably Natalie, banging pots and pans around in the kitchen.

"Natalie is making dinner now." She walked carefully up to her father's bed and sat slowly.

He narrowed his eyes at her. "Aren't you Natalie?"

Nora picked a crumb off her dad's knee. "No. I'm your daughter, Nora."

"I'm hungry."

She nodded. "Natalie is working on dinner. We'll wait here a little bit before going out there, okay?"

She wanted to give Natalie some time to relax. She'd try to give her dad a new hat as the aide suggested. If she was going to avoid Ravensbridge, she'd need to be able to show Dell she could calm him down and work with him.

"I don't know where my coat is." Her father stood and started opening doors and drawers, frowning.

"We'll be inside, so you won't need a coat." She moved to him and placed a hand tentatively on his arm. He jerked away, and she fell back. She'd never been frightened of her father before, but she realized he was taller than her. If he could hit Dell, he could hit her. "W-why don't we sit down?" She turned to a photo on his dresser and said, "This is a lovely photo. Tell me about it." She worked hard not to ask a question like "who is this?" Claire had suggested leading questions instead.

He stumbled as he made his way to her. Her dad had always been active, walking several miles a day. He would sometimes even walk the four miles to the funeral home in the morning and back at the end of the day. But that had been quite a while ago. In fact, he had rarely been out of Dell's home in the last year except for doctor's visits and church. Although he still was an imposing figure, he looked ... frail now.

"That's my wife on our wedding day," he said, taking the photo from the dresser and pulling the frame to his chest. "She's dead."

Tears welled in his eyes and Nora's too. She wasn't sure if remembering her mother's death was good or bad.

Then he put the picture down on the dresser again and turned toward the door. "I'm hungry."

Nora hastened to catch up with him, hoping Natalie and Dell had some time to calm down.

Dell looked up from the kitchen table as they entered, and Nora noticed the redness on her brother's face had shifted into a pink color. She settled her dad in a chair and went to Dell.

"Should you put something on that?" She reached out to touch the red mark, but Dell dodged her.

"Let's go into the other room. Natalie, will you be okay?"

His wife looked up from the pot she was stirring. Her gaze flitted to her father-in-law who had picked up a paper napkin and was shredding it. She nodded once. "But come back if you hear anything."

Dell placed several more napkins in front of their father. "We'll just be in the next room." He kissed his wife's temple and walked away.

Nora followed her brother back to the couch. He sank into the cushions and laid his head back against the top of the couch.

"Tell me what happened," she said.

"Dad hit me."

"Why?"

Without lifting his head, Dell turned to her, and she could see his bloodshot eyes. Although the red mark was fading, there would be a nasty bruise in the morning.

"I grabbed his arm to keep him from falling. He railed at me that a son should never attack his father. I couldn't convince him of the truth. Natalie tried to interject, to give him a 'new hat.' When he shoved her away, I grabbed him again, and he punched me." Dell reached up to lightly touch the spot and winced. "It was all very quick. He continued to yell, and the kids came. Natalie put them on the couch then came back to help me. Dad fought me the whole time as I was trying to calm him down. I didn't handle the altercation well. I guess I should have walked away. It's just so frustrating

89

when he doesn't understand. Things are so irrational with him."

"Maybe you grabbed him too hard."

It wasn't like their father to be gruff or combative. He'd never laid a hand on them as children, except when they'd needed a swat when they'd disobeyed him or their mother. But Nora could only remember being spanked with a leather strap their father kept on top of the fridge twice in her whole life.

Dell stared at her. "No, Nora. I told you he's done this before. When he doesn't remember, he gets angry."

Nora couldn't believe what she was hearing. Her father had never been a violent man. She remembered how he had come running when she fell on the ice at the age of ten and held Dell after he had been kicked by their old horse, Nugget.

"Nor, I can't keep doing this." The hitch in his voice made a lump grow in her throat. "We have to put him in the home."

Had it really come to this?

Her mind tried to think of other alternatives. Surely the home wasn't the only option. She was working with the aide, learning new things all the time.

"I still think we could hire someone. Or I could live with him. Maybe in his own house so you guys have—"

But Dell was already shaking his head. "I told you, it's too expensive. We just can't afford someone to be with him all the time. And he needs someone all the time. He falls too. A lot. He won't let us help him up. He hates being touched. Everything I do makes him mad. He'll hit you too. Eventually."

"No, I don't believe that. I'm sure we can—"

Dell stared hard at her. "He will, Nora. He's hit Natalie. He grabbed Ethan's arm. He doesn't know who you are, and this isn't always rational thinking."

Nora thought of her father's angry tone from just moments ago and how he'd shaken off her touch. "You never told me."

Dell glanced at her, wiping his hands up and down his jeans. "You were away."

Nora fell back against the couch. "That was only a week."

Dell let out a breath. "I thought I could handle it."

"I'm younger, but not a baby anymore, Dell. I'm a grown adult. I can handle tough things."

"Well, running away to the beach whenever life happens makes you look a little less than an adult."

"Ouch. That's not cool, big brother. We all deal with things—"

Dell waved her off. "I'm sorry. Forget I said that. We can't turn on each other right now." He looked at her and she nodded. "It's just that Dad has progressed so fast, and I'm so ill-equipped. One day he was just not remembering things, then he got unsteady on his feet. Every time he couldn't remember, he lashed out at one of us."

Nora was not ready for this stage of her life—the one where she and her brother became parents to their parent. Their mother had died a quick death—a sudden heart attack. She'd been able and capable until the unexpected happened. Their father had been stalwart after their mother's death, a solid oak shading them, protecting them in every season. They'd never dreamed he'd follow along so soon. Yet his death was not imminent ... at least not the physical death of his body.

Nora could feel the winter season coming when their lives would detach from the life-giving oak.

She sat forward and put her head in her hands. Dell rubbed circles on her back.

"Ravensbridge is a nice place."

Nora hated nursing homes—their smell, the sense of despair, the old people wandering aimlessly in the halls. How could she let her father go to such a place?

"Nor, it's one of the best around. And affordable. At least for now. Although we'll have to consider selling Dad's house and—"

"No!" Nora stood. "No. We will not sell Dad's house." She began to pace the living room in front of Dell. "Does Dad know we're thinking of moving him?"

Dell looked up with wet eyes. "We? So you agree?"

Nora sat down again and took her brother's hand in hers. "Your family is important, Dell. *You* are important, both to me and them. I-I can't let this go on. He's hurt you." She put a hand to the mark on his face, and he pulled back slightly before she could touch it. "This is unacceptable. Even if he has no idea what he's doing, we need help. People who are trained for this sort of thing. But we have to make educated decisions. He deserves that."

Dell fell against her, and she heard him take a sharp intake of air.

"Can I see the place, at least?" she asked.

Dell nodded against her shoulder. "I'll set something up for tomorrow. They're really nice, Nor. He'll be well cared for."

Nora wanted to believe, needed to for Dell and his family's sake, but she was still unconvinced. Yet, what choice did she have? As her brother's body shook against hers, she held tight, knowing the seasons of their life were changing whether she wanted them to or not.

Chapter Fourteen

Dell and Nora went to Ravensbridge the next morning, where a sharply dressed man greeted them at the door.

"Welcome. You must be Nora and Dell. My name is Calvin Maplethorpe." The man reached out a hand in greeting. "I'm the director of this facility. I would love to give you a tour and answer any questions you might have."

Nora followed behind the two men as they chatted, Mr. Maplethorpe pointing out the highlights of the center as they walked.

"Along this hallway are some of our rooms. Your father would be in another wing that has a bit more protection due to his level of dementia issues. This helps us to ensure his safety and the safety of the other residents."

Nora didn't like the insinuation that her father might harm others. He had never hurt a flea. She thought about Dell's bruise. This new man was not the father she knew. This was a whole new man with a whole new mindset. One they would possibly never understand.

"Can we look inside one of the rooms?" Dell asked.

Mr. Maplethorpe frowned. "Well, usually, we don't do that as the rooms are our residents' private spaces."

Dell nodded. "I understand. I just want Nora to see how nice everything is." He looked back at her. "She's having a few second thoughts about all this."

"They can check out my room, Calvin."

The trio turned to a woman pushing a walker in front of her as she meandered down the hall. Her long flowy skirt billowed around white tennis shoes. Bracelets tinkled against her wrists.

"Nora, is that you? How are you?" The woman looked through thick glasses with multicolored frames.

"Mrs. Cipriani? I didn't know you lived here."

Mrs. Cipriani had been Nora's art teacher in high school. She had been the one to first get her interested in photography and artists like Georgia O'Keefe and Ansel Adams. Nora walked up to the woman and gave her a gentle hug.

"Yes. I've been here for about four years now. A nice place if you're looking. They even let me teach some art to the other residents sometimes." She winked at Mr. Maplethorpe.

"Hazel is one of our most active residents," he said. "We are blessed to have her here. She does help with many of the activities."

"And I enjoy it. Keeps me young," she said with a twinkle in her eyes. "And sane."

Mr. Maplethorpe tsked. "Now, Hazel, you know we don't talk like that here."

She waved him off and her bracelets tinkled again. Nora remembered how Mrs. C had always been a little Bohemian.

"Why are you here if you're so active?" Nora asked.

Mrs. Cipriani lifted one shoulder. "I kept falling at my house." She jiggled the walker. "This thing helps, but my home was small and hard to get around in. These hallways are much more accommodating, and there's always someone here to help me if I fall. Not having children means you don't

94

have any help when the body starts to go." She leaned toward Nora and whispered, "And the mind isn't what it used to be either."

Nora felt a surge of emotion and some hope at her previous teacher's words. *Could Dad be happy here? Less lonely with people who understood him. People his own age?* Although he *did* have kids to help. She felt another pang of guilt take hold.

"Anyway, come this way." Mrs. Cipriani shuffled past the little group and to a closed door with all kinds of artwork covering the outside. "As you can see, my passion for art remains." She used her key to open the door, then moved inside. "Come, come. Nothing to hide here."

The group followed her into a small, but cozy, room with a bed, dresser, plush recliner, and nightstand. The dresser was full of personal supplies, makeup, hairbrushes, and two handheld mirrors. More artwork lined the walls, some without frames and some just tacked up with multicolored thumbtacks. Nora remembered that Mrs. Cipriani hadn't ever been quite organized, always telling her students that most artists were not.

"As you can see, not much has changed." Mrs. Cipriani gestured to the room and winked at Nora. "It's small but comfortable. They let me bring in my own recliner and anything else I really want. The bathroom is through there."

She pointed to another door, and Nora peeked in to see more of the chaos within. But the area was big and had safety features. She noticed the room didn't smell of old people and disease, but of lavender and vanilla.

"Dad doesn't bathe himself at this point," Dell said.

Nora turned to him and frowned. "Since when?"

Dell gave her a look before turning back to Mr. Maplethorpe. "Would he have help?"

"Oh yes. As I said, he would be in a wing that's a bit more hands on. We strive to ensure our residents are safe and well-cared for."

Mrs. Cipriani plopped down in her recliner and pushed her walker off to the side. "Nora, come here, dear."

Nora did as she was asked while the men walked to the bathroom door and talked about safety railings and non-slip, walk-in showers.

Mrs. Cipriani motioned for her to come closer, and Nora squatted down to her level.

"This is a very nice place. I do think people are happy here. I know it's a hard decision. So many people feel like this is just a place to die." She bopped her head back and forth, her once blonde but now gray curls bouncing. "Well, it is, and it isn't. But there are good people here." She reached out for Nora's hand. "They care."

"Thank you. I'm so glad you're here. Knowing there will be good people around my dad makes my heart feel a little less heavy." She smiled at her former teacher. "And the place doesn't smell as bad as some of those other homes."

Mrs. Cipriani winked. "I use a lot of essential oils to fill my place with good smells. And I may have encouraged some other residents and staff to do the same. I could help you with some for your dad." She put a finger up to her lips. "But don't tell the warden." She nodded toward the bathroom where Mr. Maplethorpe stood, and Nora giggled.

The old woman patted an ottoman next to her and Nora took a seat.

"Do you still work on your art, dear? I remember you had a gift for photography."

Her mind still seems intact. How could she remember one student's hobby out of thousands she must have taught over the years?

Nora smiled. "I got away from the hobby for a bit, but I'm getting back into it. I just bought some new accessories for my camera."

"Oh, how exciting." Mrs. C clapped her hands, setting the bracelets tinkling again. Nora noticed every finger was covered in eclectic rings too. "You will have to come back and show me some of your work."

Nora promised to do so as Dell and Mr. Maplethorpe came out from the bathroom.

"Thank you, Hazel, for this generous offer of showing off your place, but we'll get out of your hair now." Mr. Maplethorpe nodded to Hazel as he moved toward the door.

"No problem, Calvin. I'm happy to help, especially to one of my former students." She patted Nora's hand and smiled.

As the trio walked back into the hallway, Mrs. Cipriani called out, "Calvin, how about some chocolate pudding for dinner tonight?"

"I'll see what I can do," he called back, closing her door with a soft click.

He brought them to a wall made entirely of glass. Inside, Nora could see many residents playing board games, cards, and a pair simulating bowling being guided by a computer-generated player on a large TV screen.

"As you can see, we try to offer as many stimulating activities as we can. We also do take into consideration those with issues similar to your father's—to their mental capacity. We have games that engage our residents' brain while also being fun. And as Mrs. Cipriani said, we let her give some art classes. Mostly just fingerpaints or watercolors."

"This is outside the memory care wing, though, right?" Dell asked.

Mr. Maplethorpe nodded, but said, "This games room is, yes, but there is another just like it in the other wing." He motioned down the hallway. "Let's go into the memory care wing so you can see that space."

At the end of the hallway, they walked through several locked doors, Mr. Maplethorpe using the key attached to a chain at his waist to enter. Once the doors were locked behind them, Mr. Maplethorpe kept walking.

They passed a display with an old, black rotary phone sitting on a pretty doily on top of an antique side table. Next to the table sat an old Singer sewing machine in its cabinet with what looked to be a 1920s, elegant dress on a dress form.

"What's this?" Nora asked.

"We use some antique items displayed throughout this wing to help trigger pleasant memories for the residents. Some of them like to sit and reminisce. Dementia patients are all different but can often recall things from their youth better than the most recent ones."

Mr. Maplethorpe walked to another hallway with a door that led to an outside courtyard. "Here is a safe space for all residents to enjoy the outdoors. Completely enclosed so they would have to go through the building to get outside the complex. All the doors have alarms that ring back to main stations as well as cameras for our staff to monitor." He pointed to a nondescript apparatus hanging from the eaves.

Just like jail. Dad would be confined. Unable to talk to the outside world. Unable to see friends.

Their father had always been engaging and friendly— most funeral home directors needed to be, simply to dispel the Vincent Price aura.

Nora looked around the courtyard. There was a bench where she could see her and her father sitting. At least they could pretend they were back home. The tree reminded her of the one that used to be in their yard when she was growing up.

"Nor?"

She turned to look at her brother and Mr. Maplethorpe, who looked as though someone had asked a question.

"I'm sorry. My mind was elsewhere. Did you say something?"

"I asked what you thought. Mr. Maplethorpe says they may have a vacancy soon."

A vacancy. Just like the funeral home business. Death kept this business moving forward. The thought made her stomach turn. She put a hand to her mouth and turned away from the men, thinking again of Dell's bruise, his sobs, and the frightened look on Natalie's face when left alone with her father. And she also thought of Mrs. Cipriani who seemed content here. Perhaps she and her father could be friends even.

"Yes." Nora turned back to the men. "I think Dad will be happy here."

He wouldn't, but she needed to think of the future now. The one without her dad as the strong, driving force in the family. Now their future was up to her and her brother to command.

Forgive me, Dad.

Chapter Fifteen

Nora watched as Sarah arranged her family like a professional organizer around her grandfather, who now sat stately under the giant oak in their front yard. Sarah's mother had been able to get away only for a few days, so they'd decided on the Friday after the debacle dinner. Nora hoped neither Luke nor Sarah would ask awkward questions about Jake.

She'd spent the last few days with her father, trying to figure out a way around the nursing home move. He'd done well with the aide, but Dell had told her of another altercation they'd had with him yesterday. Nora now hoped the facility would call soon with a vacancy.

Bud had been out of bed when Nora arrived a half hour ago, ready and willing to get the pictures done. Sarah's husband Brian had moved a plush Victorian-style chair with red velvet cushions—a lot like the ones they still used at the funeral home—under the tree as Sarah and Luke had led their grandfather across the lawn. Two of Sarah's boys now stood on either side of Bud, fidgeting with their fancy clothes.

Nora snapped off a couple of photos of the chaos. When Sarah's oldest boy punched the arm of the middle boy, she caught that on film too. *Evidence for later.* Sarah might not want these shots in a frame but would love to see them and maybe have a few printed for blackmail purposes. Or for their wedding day.

Luke stood next to Nora watching the chaos, while his mom offered suggestions to Sarah and the boys.

"I think Mom is making things worse," Luke said in her ear, causing a shiver to race up her spine.

She laughed. "Ya think?" Nora watched as Sarah and Luke's mom moved one of the boys to another spot just as Sarah had gotten him to stand still. "She's just trying to help, though."

"Oh, for sure, but they're two peas in a pod—organizers. They can't help themselves. But they rarely agree on these kinds of things. We'll be lucky to get out of this without a fight today."

"Well, isn't your job to play referee?" Nora glanced at him and smirked, before snapping a pic of Bud who was clearly enjoying his great grandchildren's shenanigans. He simply sat in his fancy chair and smiled. Occasionally he would laugh, and Nora would snap a pic. These would be priceless later.

"Oh, trust me. Brian and I have a whole silent look thing going on right now. If I'm needed, I'm ready to jump into action."

Nora turned and snapped a pic of Luke then, causing him to turn to her with eyebrows raised.

"Thought I might get one of those silent looks on camera." She smiled.

"Okay," Sarah said, finally corralling the boys in the appropriate spots while fending off her mother's attempts to rearrange things. "I think we're ready." She stood in front of the group surveying her family, dressed in their finest slacks and button-down shirts. She had ensured they all wore a similar color palette.

"Um, Sarah?" Luke said.

Sarah turned to look at him. "Yeah?"

"You need to be in the pic, Sis."

Sarah's eye grew wide, and she laughed. "Oops. You're right. Okay, I'll be beside Brian. How's this?" She snuggled up close to her husband. He put his arm around her and looked down lovingly.

Nora quickly snapped a pic while they were lost in each other's eyes. She noticed the youngest son, on Bud's lap, starting to grow fussy.

"Okay, folks, eyes up here. Sarah, hold your right hand to your thigh ... good. Tim put your left hand in your pocket. Perfect. Now everybody, look up here and smile."

The shutter sound on her camera clicked away as she snapped off a succession of photos. She consulted the digital screen. *Good.* She'd read a bunch of articles over the last week about poses and how to interact with photography clients. As she looked at each shot, she felt good about this new endeavor.

"Luke, you and your mom need to get in there next. Hey, Tim and Ian! Stand still. We'll be done soon."

Nora waited as Luke and his mom took up spots behind the boys—both to be in the shots and to hold the squirrely youngsters in place. She snapped off more photos as she offered instructions for each person.

"Let's get a couple with just Bud and the kids." She knew to get the kids' photos out of the way first because they would grow antsy if asked to sit still for too long. As the other adults stepped away, Nora asked the kids to lean in and she snapped off more pics. She wanted to have plenty to choose from. She felt nervous and had barely slept last night, wanting to do a good job today. As she fought to use the sunlight to her advantage, she made a note to purchase a light stand for any future photoshoots. She couldn't rely on every time being this sunny and warm, especially since the days were wending further into fall.

A few leaves fluttered down off the tree, and Nora snapped a series of photos, catching the leaves in just the right composition around the family.

"Tim, stop pinching your brother!" Sarah yelled, bringing Nora back into the moment.

"Almost done, boys. Ian, can you move just slightly to your right? Your other right. Stop! That's perfect." Nora fired off a few more shots before telling the boys they could step away.

"Now Sarah, Luke, and Mom, get back in there. Sarah, what if you squat down beside Bud with the baby and Luke and your mom stand behind?" The couple did as she asked. "Luke, just come a bit to your right so you're at the edge of the—perfect! And put your left hand in your pocket. Good."

Nora brought the viewfinder up to her face and snapped a few more. One, she was sure, even had the baby smiling at her. As she continued to hit the button on her camera, her gaze stayed locked on Luke through the viewfinder. Today, he looked even more handsome than he had the other night at dinner. And he smelled good too. She had noticed his subtle cologne as he stood next to her earlier.

When she saw Sarah make an angry face to someone off camera, Nora knew they needed to move on.

Luke and Brain moved Bud to the porch next and went through another round of shots before Bud announced he was feeling worn out. Sarah's mother quickly ushered the boys and the baby inside while Luke and Brian helped Bud back to his bed.

"Everybody out while I get Gramps comfortable," Sarah announced, shooing everyone away.

"Sarah, I'll get out of your hair—" Nora started to say.

"Oh no. You come here." Sarah waved her closer to the edge of Bud's bed. When the others were gone from the room, she said, "I would like a few of just me and Gramps. And maybe just a few of him." She turned to her grandfather. "Are you okay with that? You don't even need to keep your eyes open if you don't want to."

Bud nodded. "I'm back in bed now and can rest. Do what you need to do, my dear."

Sarah ran her thumb over the back of Bud's hand as she gazed down at him. Finally, she turned back to Nora. "These will be just for me. I just want something ... you understand? The shots don't have to be picture perfect."

Nora nodded and Sarah bent down beside Bud's bed. When she looked at him, Nora snapped a photo. When he turned to her and smiled, she snapped another. When Bud took Sarah's hand and kissed it, *snap*. Nora felt their emotion through the camera, and she fought back tears.

After taking about twenty more photos of the two and some just of their hands entwined, she declared the session done. Bud closed his eyes, spent from his modeling time. Sarah and Nora watched for a few minutes without speaking or moving. When they noticed Bud's breathing had grown steady, Nora took one last picture and Sarah stood.

"He's asleep." Sarah waved her away from the bed.

"I'll be going then," Nora whispered.

Sarah frowned. "No, you will not. I made lunch, and you are going to stay and enjoy it. Well, you will hopefully enjoy the food, I don't know about my brood." She laughed, nudging Nora in the direction of the other room.

As they entered the kitchen, Nora took in the scene. Tim on Luke's knee and Ian on Brian's as they each watched something on their cell phones.

Brian looked up as Sarah approached. "Your mom is putting the baby down. He was pooped—both literally and figuratively."

Sarah kissed the top of Ian's head, then her husband's. "Thanks, babe. What are you guys watching?"

"Penn game," Tim said without looking away from the screen.

"I thought Penn State played tomorrow," Nora said.

"No, *Penn*. Not Penn State."

The five-year-old's exasperated tone made Nora smile, but Sarah was not impressed.

"Hey, kid. Watch that tone or you won't be watching any football." She moved to the fridge and began pulling out food.

"Sorry, Mom."

Luke ruffled his nephew's hair before turning to Nora with a smile. "Staying for lunch, I hope?"

"Sarah pretty much told me doing so was required."

Nora put her camera in her bag and stashed it in a safe place. When she returned to the kitchen, Sarah handed Nora a stack of plates and she moved to the table to set them down.

"Boys, time to give up the table. We're going to eat lunch," Sarah called over her shoulder as she scooped chicken salad from a container into a glass serving dish.

The kids moaned, but Brian removed the electronic devices and sat each boy at his place at the table.

"Sit next to me, Nora!" Tim indicated the chair next to his own.

"Well, I have never felt so special," Nora said as she took her seat directly across from Luke.

He smiled at her, then turned to Sarah. "Need any help, Sis?"

"You know she doesn't," Brian told him. "Harriet Homemaker has everything all planned out. Just stay in your seat."

Sarah moved to the table and made a face at her husband. "I just like to entertain, that's all. Now everybody sit, and I'll go get Mom."

Sarah bustled from the room as the rest did as they were told. When Ian reached for the rolls, Brian grabbed his hand and shook his head. "We have to wait until Mom and Grandma get back, little man. And we need to pray. You know better."

Ian crossed his arms and sat back in his chair, pouting.

After Sarah and her mother had returned and taken their seats, Brian told everyone to bow their heads for prayer.

"Dear heavenly Father, we are so thankful for your loving ways and for the gift of family. Thank you, Lord, for these days with Bud, for Luke and Mom's ability to be here during this time, and for Nora's special gift of photography, so we will have these moments to look back on forever. Thank you, too, for this food and the hands that prepared it. May it be nourishing to our bodies as your Word is nourishment to our souls. We are so thankful for you, Lord, and for the Son you have provided for us. In Jesus's most precious and holy name, amen."

The others echoed the amen, then dug in.

Nora watched as others filled their plates with rolls and salad, wondering about Brian's prayer. She had never thought of knowing how to photograph people as a gift. She'd just been looking to make something of her own and had taught herself some things. She thought of Mrs. Cipriani again and how she'd been the best art teacher. She'd had a gift. And of the aide ... Claire. She was so patient and kind with Dad when he was grumpy. Even when Nora was getting flustered, Claire stayed calm. She had a gift. Photography certainly was something she loved as a hobby—did that make it her gift? As she tucked into her meal, she smiled.

Now, to just get this business off the ground.

Chapter Sixteen

After lunch, she returned to the funeral home. The quiet hush of the old Victorian home greeted her as she closed the door behind her. She sighed and turned toward her office door. She wanted to go through the images on her camera right away so she wouldn't lose the feeling she had while taking them.

She sank into the plush office chair and opened the viewfinder. She smiled as she clicked through each one and laughed at the boys' antics. Sarah would love these. These photos were more than just about Bud—they were about a family.

She came across one with Luke, Sarah, and Bud she couldn't move past. She'd spent almost the entire day with them and loved how they'd interacted as a family. They'd barely had any arguments and didn't seem like they were hiding anything. She had seen how grief could exacerbate familial issues, but the Hoffmasters seemed to be taking the imminent loss of Bud well. His illness had brought them together. She hoped this trial with her father wouldn't tear her and Dell apart. They needed each other.

As she clicked through each image, she made notes on a piece of paper about which ones she felt were best to send to

Sarah. Of course, she'd give Sarah all the photos on a flash drive, but she wanted to send a few select ones to her that centered around Bud first.

When she came to the last photo, she made a few more notes on her paper before setting the camera down. She felt worn out from interacting today, and she'd realized just how much she could have done had she had a place to photograph the Hoffmasters instead of doing the shoot outside. What if the day had been rainy or snowing? What would she do in cold weather times?

Perhaps she needed a storefront. She had seen one downtown earlier and jotted down the number. She dug the slip of paper out of her purse and called.

A few minutes later, she ended the call with a sigh. She could never afford the rent they were asking, especially until she got a few more jobs under her belt.

She looked back at the camera again. *How can I make this work?*

She focused her attention on the stack of paperwork before her. Ads, catalogs, invoices ... how did Dad keep everything straight?

Is this piece of mail about their coffin insurance real or a scam? Do we really spend this much on electricity? How many catalogs do they need for supplies?

She flipped through one catalog and cringed when she saw the embalming fluid and various apparatus needed.

Thank goodness Dell handles that part of the business.

She shuffled through a few more envelopes, making two piles—one for items she knew she needed to address and one to ask her brother about.

Where was Dell anyway?

She knew he should be here somewhere, but the place remained quiet. They didn't have any funerals this week, but Dell had mentioned he'd be at the office today.

She rose from her desk and walked out to the main lobby. She knew almost every room but had rarely gone upstairs. She considered the stairs leading to the second floor that stood right outside her office door. Was Dell up there? She didn't think so. The second floor was mostly used for storage. She turned instead to the left and into the main viewing room. She clicked on the lights that cast a warm, pink hue up the walls and wondered again if they should do a bit of updating. The Victorian furniture made the place look dated, but her dad had always said people liked the warm tones of the dark wood and plush fabric.

She walked through the room to the connecting one, pushing aside the pocket doors into a smaller sitting room. This was where the bereaved often gathered for a bit before greeting other mourners. She checked to ensure the tissue boxes were still mostly full, then moved into the back room.

Once a kitchen in the house, a small countertop with a coffee maker, toaster oven, and hot plate remained with a small round table and four chairs. She hadn't yet stayed long enough to have lunch here. Something about having lunch in a funeral home felt off to her.

She turned back into the main room and ran smack into her brother. She let out a little squeak.

Dell didn't reach out for her arms to steady her but looked down with a scowl. "You were gone a long time."

Nora consulted her phone, surprised to see the time. If she were going to balance two jobs, she'd have to get better at time management.

"First, why are you so quiet? Make a little noise next time."

Dell smiled down at her. "My stealth is one of my gifts."

She rolled her eyes. "Well, sorry I was gone longer than expected. Sarah invited me for lunch after I took the pictures, and I stayed to get to know them all better."

"I thought we were going to go through more files."

"I was looking for you for just that purpose. I have a stack of stuff in my office that needs to be addressed."

Dell nodded once. "Bring the whole pile back to my office, and we'll go through it."

An hour and a half later, Dell and Nora had gone through most of the "everyday" expenses of running a funeral home, which were more than she had ever imagined. Caskets, outer burial containers, vaults, embalming fluid, rubber gloves and other protective equipment, stationary like register books, memorial folders, thank you cards, and everything needed for the hearse they owned—insurance, registration, and upkeep. The whole mess amounted to more than Nora felt she could ever keep up with.

"This is the company we use for some of the main things," Dell said as he handed her a catalog from Hilton Funeral Supply.

This company sold almost everything any funeral home could need down to keepsake ornaments and promotional items for the business.

"It seems odd to advertise, doesn't it?" she asked.

Dell handed her a pen with Harper Funeral Home printed on the side with their phone number. "Dad gives those away when someone signs a contract with us or when he meets with a family. You should have taken some with you today."

Nora turned the lightweight pen around in her hand. She should have given one to the Hoffmasters. Although she knew they would be using their services anyway.

"Where do we keep these?" she asked.

"There should be some in Dad's ... your office. Maybe in a box. I can find them for you later, if you want."

She waved the pen at him. "Never mind. I can look. But don't you think these things feel ... icky?"

"Dad was always mindful of not being ... salesy, but it's still a business," Dell said, looking at her over the top of his reading glasses.

She agreed. "It seems very gauche to be pushy. People in Millsburgh know we're here."

Dell nodded. She was glad they were finally on the same page about something. He really did know quite a bit and was obviously an integral part of their family's business.

Dell flipped through the catalog and held it out toward her, a page of urns showing. "Here are the urns we normally buy. Okay if I get some more ordered?"

She nodded. "Do what you think is best."

"What about ordering a few in this color too?" He pointed to a pewter colored vase. "We normally only have the gold color, but some people have expressed wanting an option." He pulled the catalog back to look at the page again. "Although we can always just order one for them."

"Get a few to have on hand. It's nice to be able to offer something right away, yes?"

He nodded and made a note on a piece of sticky paper. "Dell?"

He offered a grunt but didn't look up.

"Dell? Can you please look at me?"

He looked up again over his glasses.

"Do you think we're doing the right thing with Dad?"

Dell sighed. "You're not backing out, are you? I already made a down payment. Seriously, Nor—"

She held out a hand to her brother. "No. It's fine. I mean ... yes, I hate it." She sat back in the chair across from his desk. "It's just a lot of things will need to change soon, and I'm not ready for them."

Dell sat back in his chair too, mirroring her stance. "Want to tell me about your dinner with Jake?"

"It was ... we ... I think I need some coffee first. You?"

Dell nodded and she moved back to the kitchen and brewed a pot. She knew she was stalling, but she didn't know why.

When the pot burbled its last drip, she filled two mugs and returned to Dell's office.

"Okay," he said, sitting back in his chair with mug in hand, "tell me what you're really thinking."

She loved how her brother knew her so well.

She sighed as she warmed her cold fingers on the coffee mug. "Jake was late—at least by my estimation. We ran into Sarah and her brother Luke, so they joined us. I wished they hadn't, though. Jake got upset when I mentioned the photography thing and told me he'd bought us a house in Vermont."

"Vermont?" Dell sat forward, nearly spilling his coffee. "What the ... you were going to move? Nora, I really need you he—"

She held up a hand. "He hadn't told me, Dell. Just made plans on his own. Thought his idea would make me happy."

Dell sat back in his chair. "And ... would it?"

She scrunched up her face at him. "No. I wouldn't leave you and Dad. Be serious."

"I don't know with you lately. Running off to the beach, wanting to start your own business ..."

"Jake realized making decisions without me wasn't the right thing to do," she said, ignoring her brother's jabs. "After I stormed out of the restaurant, he followed me home, and we broke up. For good this time."

"Yeah, right. You guys go back and forth. What makes this time different?"

"Well, he's still moving to Vermont for one. He's taking over the business up there from his uncle."

Dell nodded and sipped his coffee.

"You're not mad?" she asked him.

Dell frowned. "Why would I be mad?"

"Well, he's your friend and this might, I don't know, affect that."

"Nor, you are my sister. Family comes first." He reached over the desk and held out his hand. She took it in her own. "Jake and I aren't best friends or anything. He's gotta do what he needs to do and so do we."

She smiled and wiped a tear from her cheek.

Dell offered her a wide grin and let go of her hand. "It's almost time for dinner. Natalie is cooking her famous meatloaf. Want to come?"

"Nah, I need to get home and go through these pictures for Sarah."

"I'll bring you some later then."

"That would be nice. Thanks." She rose from the chair and walked toward the door. As she opened it, she turned back to her brother and said, "Is this business what you want?" she whispered, not truly sure if she wanted his answer.

He looked at her for a full minute before saying, "It's my duty."

"You could decide to do something else."

"Like what? This is all I know. And I like doing this. It's a service to the people here. People I know and love."

"But don't you want to find your own purpose?"

"What if this is my purpose? Aren't we called to simply love one another, do as Christ did for one another? That's my purpose ... to help people when their loved ones die. I find joy in this, Nor. I'm sorry you don't."

Brother and sister stared at each other for a few more seconds before Nora moved through the door and closed it softly behind her.

She didn't feel the same way but understood what her brother was saying.

As she moved back to her office, she looked up the stairs to the second floor again.

Maybe tomorrow I'll check out what's up there.

Chapter Seventeen

The next few weeks flew by in a blur, and Nora had not a single moment to think about starting her new business or finding her purpose as she and Dell handled several unexpected funerals.

In addition, Ravensbridge's director had called them to say they had a room available for their father. She and Dell had spent a few days gathering things from Dad's house that would make him feel more at home. Although they'd tried to talk with their father about the move, he never quite seemed to understand, which made Nora feel even worse about the decision. She kept coming up with more ways to keep him at home, but, in the end, when her father had continued to become heated and angry, she'd given up.

Then her mind moved to new worries.

What if his dementia worsens due to the move? What if he just stays in his room every day, alone and feeling abandoned? What if he dies soon?

Nora could only hope and pray they would make this work. That the move would be good for their father and the entire family.

The day of the move, Nora and Dell had done all the heavy lifting, which was not much since they could only take a few furniture items for the small room. Her dad's clothes had been the hardest part. Since winter would be arriving soon, some days were still warm, so they had packed some light knit items and also heavier sweaters. Who knew what the temperature might be like on a daily basis in the center. They tried to pack for every contingency, which had resulted in more clothes than they could fit in the tiny closet.

When they had left their dad a few days ago, Nora and Dell had both shed a few tears in the parking lot before heading back home.

Nora felt like everything was moving too fast, her life hurtling past her. She'd still not made progress in her photography business. How could she, with all that was now needed from her—more funerals than they could handle, keeping up with the daily tasks at the funeral home, and trying to clear out the rest of their father's home.

She called Gabe in the Outer Banks in a small moment of time she had. When her friend answered, with a smile in his voice, she felt instantly more relaxed.

"Hey, yourself. How are things in sunny North Carolina?" she asked, sitting back on her plush couch with a hot cup of tea.

"Not bad. Not that sunny anymore here, though. Although more than PA, I imagine. How goes the new business?"

She snorted. "It doesn't. I haven't even had a moment to figure out how to get started. I need business cards, and I'll need to do some advertising. I did get a small gig photographing a newborn, but I really didn't have the props I needed or the space to set things up properly. I really need a space, but everything is so expensive."

"Maybe you could use your dad's house? He is moved out, right?"

Nora thought of the idea for a moment before saying, "I don't know if Dell would appreciate that. And everything is a mess in there right now. We're trying to decide what stays and what goes. It's quite the process."

"You'll figure something out. If this is what God wants you to do, he'll make a way."

Nora took a sip of her tea, letting the warm liquid tickle down her throat. "I feel a little like a failure. I'm in my forties and haven't figured out God's plan for me yet."

"Maybe you should be listening to him more instead of trying to figure everything out yourself," Gabe suggested.

"Well, I have prayed. Maybe he's upset that I've wasted so much of my life. I could have been figuring this out a long time ago."

"To everything there is a season," Gabe quoted the familiar verse she'd heard a few weeks ago in church. "Your season is changing just like the leaves on the trees outside. Our lives ebb and flow like the seasons and the tide, remember? So many people see autumn as the death of things, but the plants and trees come back to spring and life eventually, right? And sometimes we need the end of things to come before we can restart fresh. Like Ellie dying and your dad's decline into dementia. Maybe it just wasn't the right season for you until now."

"It feels a little uncomfortable ... not knowing what might come next," she confided.

"Oh, trust me. I get that."

They both laughed.

After a moment of silence, Gabe said, "But when I let God direct my steps here, and when I finally let go of my own fears, things got kind of exciting. I never dreamed I'd be running this kind of business now—books and coffee. But I am having so much fun. Sometimes the unknown is exciting, not scary. Aren't you excited to see what God will do with this gift? Where he will take you if you just let him, trust in him, follow his lead?"

"My mom used to always say, 'If it's God's way, it's an easy way.'"

"Well, living for the Lord is not really an easy life," Gabe said.

"No, it's not. But she believed if you were in God's will, stuff just felt into place rapidly. Like, there wouldn't be any hinderances. I feel like I'm pushing against something. Like I've not quite hit the sweet spot. Does that make sense?"

"Oh, absolutely. When Ellie and I had to make any big decisions, we'd pray over them and talk about what each of us were feeling. If we had similar feelings, we knew the idea was probably from God. If we disagreed or something didn't seem to fit, like you're saying, we prayed more or didn't act until we were sure. Usually, things had a way of working out either way."

"I've been praying, but I'm not hearing God's voice or any nudging in a particular direction." Nora sighed. "Maybe starting a photography business isn't God's will for me. I just don't feel settled. I'm not living my own life, but the life of others."

"I understand that too," Gabe said. "I lived a lot of my life for Ellie, and I didn't know what to do with myself when she died. Now, with my new business here with Gladys, I really feel like I'm coming into my own. You'll find that too, just keep talking to God about it."

They talked for a bit more before ending the conversation. Nora promised to call him again when things calmed down a little. As she finished the last of her now lukewarm tea, she felt glad God had brought Gabe into her life. He'd become a good friend in a really short period of time. She had seen his faith reborn too. He'd begun attending church every Sunday and had talked about God in almost all their conversations.

She laid her head on the couch's back and closed her eyes.

Lord, I don't want life to pass me by. I don't want to simply do what others have done. I want to find my own path, my own purpose. I like helping others, and I love photography. How can I combine them? Please show me the path.

Nora entered Ravenbridge's memory care building a few hours later. She and Dell had tried to visit their father every day, taking turns so as not to burn out. Today was her day, but she wasn't looking forward to it.

As she entered Ravensbridge LIFE Center—*why don't they call them nursing homes anymore?*—her nose immediately wrinkled at the smell. *And why do they always smell so bad?*

"Welcome back, Nora," the front desk clerk, Susie, greeted.

"Hey, Susie. Is he in his room?"

Her father hadn't ventured much out of his room yet, but she hoped he might soon. The last two times she had visited, he had barely spoken to her, obviously mad about the move. She was already growing to hate the visits and hoped she might get more accustomed to them—and her father to his new home—in time.

"Ah ... no," Susie finally answered her. "He's been hanging out in the games room today."

Finally. Maybe this was the progress she was hoping for. Maybe today would be a good visit.

"Thanks."

Susie pressed the button for Nora to enter, and the door made a clicking sound before swinging open. The door snapped shut behind her and another door opened a few steps ahead. Again, she was reminded of a prison.

As Nora walked down the brightly lit hallway, she passed other patients—*residents*—of the home. Many sat in wheelchairs, vacant looks in their eyes. Nora couldn't stand to see so many people left behind, all sense of themselves seemingly lost to time. Especially here in the memory care unit where all the residents were fighting some form of dementia.

She hated that her father had to live here now. She rarely saw other families visiting. A fact she found sad despite her own disinterest in being here. She knew visiting was hard when your loved one might not acknowledge you or want to talk. So many people with dementia were non-verbal. She was glad her father could still talk about some things.

But she couldn't just let her dad waste away here, his mind increasingly deteriorating. At least here he got good meals and someone to dress and bathe him regularly—a task that had become too much for her and Dell as well.

She felt like a failure. Who couldn't even take care of their loved one? But their dad's quick decline into dementia had caught them both off guard. He had been a strong-willed and quick witted man before the disease began to eat away at his memories and confuse his mind.

She hoped he could establish a routine here soon. Hoped he would begin to have better days. Although, she knew the progression of the disease didn't allow for that. There would be no more *better* days mentally. But she hoped he would grow to like the place at the very least. Perhaps befriend one or two of these folks sitting alone in the hallway.

She stepped into the games room just in time to see her father fling a board game across the room, small pieces and cards flying. A large man in medical scrubs quickly restrained her father as Nora stood gaping.

"Mr. Harper ... Ned! We can't simply throw stuff when things aren't going our way, man."

Nora watched for a moment as the man struggled with her father. Despite the attendant's size, her father was winning the battle. *He always was a strong man.*

Nora dropped her purse on the floor and ran to help.

"Dad! Hey, look at me." She put her hands on either side of his face as the attendant held his arms behind him. "It's me, Nora. Your daughter. I came to see you. How about we go take a walk?"

Her father visibly relaxed as he gazed at her face, seeming to recognize her. The large man holding him released part of his grip.

They had good and bad moments these days. Sometimes her father knew her and other times ... he had no clue. Those times hurt Nora, but she had learned his memory lapses were simply the disease, not his lack of love for her.

"Thanks ... John," she said, reading the attendant's name tag. "I can take him from here."

Before releasing her father's arms fully, John asked, "You sure? He's been a bit riled up today."

She nodded, and John let him go. Her father scowled at him as he brushed off his sleeves. John stared intently, ready to jump into action again if needed.

Nora put her arm through the crook of her father's arm. "We'll be fine, right Dad? Say thank you to John."

"He tried to break my arm!"

"I can't wait to go sit outside with you. What do you say? Are you ready?"

Although she'd never encountered this side of her father, she thought back to the "new hat" idea she'd been taught by Claire. She hoped redirecting his thoughts to before this altercation would be enough.

"Oh, yes. I would like that." Her father's entire being lost its tension as he looked back to the other man. "Thank you, John, for a rousing game." Nora marveled at the way her redirection had taken the starch right out of the moment. "Same time tomorrow?"

John sighed. "Perhaps. I'll let you know."

Nora mouthed "thank you" and "I'm sorry" to John. He waved his hand dismissively and bent to pick up the pieces of the board game.

She pulled at her dad's arm as he angled for the building's main entrance. "Let's go to the courtyard. The door is over here." She'd learned too not to chastise or correct but to simply offer ideas he would agree to.

"I'd like to go home, Nora."

"I know, Dad, but we can't. I ... I'm sure you just had a misunderstanding with John."

"Who's John?" Her father frowned.

Right. That moment has passed.

Nora took a deep breath and pulled her father again toward the courtyard doors. "Never mind. Let's go out to the courtyard and get some fresh air."

She thought again about how the aide had taught her to acknowledge Dad's emotion but redirect him.

"I want to *go home*." Her father planted his feet firmly.

She hesitated for a moment as she caught his firm tone. Would he hit her too? He had never struck her or even gotten that angry with her, but there was a first time for everything. She needed to tread lightly.

"I really want to see the tree in the courtyard. Would you sit with me?"

Her father hesitated, scowling again as he looked toward the front entrance. Finally, he turned to her and said, "Okay, but then we'll go home."

She nodded and steered her father toward the courtyard door, hoping he'd let go of this line of thinking while they enjoyed some late fall sunshine. She entered a code for the door to unlock, and they stepped out into the bright autumn day. They had been having a warm spell, for which she was not mad. The day was a perfect one to sit outside and enjoy some nature.

Once outside, she pointed him to a bench beneath an oak tree, its leaves having turned a vibrant yellow. A small pile of the leaves lay at the base of the tree, their brittle layers crunching as they made their way toward the bench. Her dad sat, spine straight and scowl in place until she sat next to him and gently put her hand over his.

He turned to her and frowned, then looked up at the leaves. "This tree looks dead."

She leaned her head onto his shoulder, glad he had moved on from the incident inside. "It's just autumn, when the leaves fall off and the tree rests for the winter. It'll regrow its leaves in the spring."

"I should get back to the store. Old Mrs. Peters needs to talk to me about her husband's service."

Dad always called the funeral home the store, which made her shiver. What did they sell? And who was Mrs. Peters? The old woman who used to live down the block from them? She'd died in the nineties.

"Dell and I have everything under control at the st—funeral home."

Her dad harrumphed, then kissed the top of her head. For a moment, she felt all was right with the world and she felt her body relax. She longed to still be his little girl. To shirk off responsibilities for lighter, more carefree things. To fall back into the safety and security of his arms as she had when she was a child.

"But you can help me with something," she said, hoping for a bit of clarity.

"You should talk with your mother. She knows all about girl things. Besides, I told Mrs. Peters I'd stop by today to finalize her funeral plans."

She sighed, longing to have normal conversations with her father.

"Dad, Mom is ..." She paused, knowing bringing up her dead mother would invite big emotions. "You're retired. Dell is running the business now. I help him."

Her father scoffed. "You couldn't run the business, sweet pea. You're just a kid."

Oh, how she longed for that to be true. Although not a kid anymore, she did feel ill equipped to run the business.

She thought about correcting her father, but the doctors had told them not to fight some of these things, so she chose not to now. Instead, she gave into his fantasy.

"You're right, Dad. I'm still young." The statement wasn't a full lie. "But I want to be like you, you know. A strong businessperson. Someone people look up to, who people trust. A person to be admired in the community."

He kissed the top of her head again. "You will someday, Nora girl. But for now, just enjoy your childhood."

She sighed against his shoulder. "I really want to start my own photography business, but doing so seems so hard. I can't even find a place to rent to make my studio, everything is so expensive. You had it easy when you started at the funeral home, everything was already set up for you."

Her father didn't say anything for a long while, and she wondered if he had even heard her or understood. She remained quiet too, simply enjoying the feel of the sun on her face.

"I didn't have it easy."

She looked at her father and noticed a few tears beginning to form in his eyes.

"Why not? You had the location, an established business—"

Her father snorted. "My dad's business, not mine. Everyone compares me to him. If I try to do something different, people complain. But I need to do things my way."

She noticed he was speaking in the present tense but let the words slide. Especially since he was saying almost the same things she had been feeling.

"So how did you make the business your own?" she asked.

"I just try to be loving, take interest in their grief, show them I care. Dad didn't like the idea of going to their houses. He wanted people to come to him. He liked to sit behind the desk and fill out the paperwork. But I like going to them. They have enough on their plate."

Nora had never known this tidbit about the business. She'd always assumed that's just the way things worked. Again, she wondered how she might make the funeral business her own if the photography didn't work out.

"You want to take photos?" her father said, looking at her with a frown.

"Yes, but I need a studio. It's difficult when people don't have the space at their own homes, and I can't always take pictures outside. It'll be winter soon."

Her father looked up at the tree again. "The upstairs has lots of space."

Nora looked up at the tree. Was he seeing something she wasn't? An idea dawned on her. The upstairs. At the funeral home. They hadn't used that space in years. She'd been meaning to go up there, but her life had been so busy she'd forgotten all about it.

"Is this our tree?" her father asked, still looking up at the falling leaves.

"No, Dad. This is not our tree."

In fact, they'd had to tear down the old tree a few years ago when lightning had struck the old trunk and split the oak in two, sending the now very old tire swing to the ground. She had cried when the tree surgeons had cut up its fine limbs and hauled them away.

"I wish they had a swing you could push me on here, Dad. Remember the old tire swing we had in the yard?"

"What's to remember? It's still there. We can go now if you want, and I'll push you until the sun sets."

If only there were still a swing. If only she could still fit inside it. The old tire had hung from that tree in their front yard on a long, ratty rope. Her mother had squawked every time her father had taken her and Dell out there, saying the rope or the limb would break any day. But Dad had always waved her off. Yet Nora knew how he pulled on the rope each time before letting them climb up to start their swing. He knew how to take care of them.

She brushed a tear away from the corner of her eye and turned to her father. He looked up at the tree above them now, frowning once more.

"I'm cold. Could you ask your mother to bring me a sweater?"

She wondered if they would ever understand how this disease affected people. Why one minute they were present when the next they were not.

Nora took a deep breath and said, "Okay, Dad. Let's go in."

Chapter Eighteen

On the way back to her father's room, they ran into Mrs. C, her old art teacher.

"Mrs. C, what are you doing in this part of the facility?" Nora asked.

"Oh, I give an art class here once a week. Sometimes being creative helps with the resident's ..." She glanced at Nora's father but let her thought trail off.

"I understand." She looked at her father. "Dad, this is Mrs. Cipriani, my old art teacher."

"Nice to meet you. Nora, I'm hungry."

Nora offered a sad smile to Mrs. C. "I guess I better get him to the dining room. It's nice to see you."

"I was actually just heading to the dining room here. My friend is in this wing, and we eat together sometimes. Are you staying, Nora?"

She hadn't thought of doing so, but would like to spend more time with Mrs. C. Maybe she could give her some ideas about the photography business.

"Sure, why not."

The trio headed down the hallway to the dining room, where other residents had already begun to gather. A woman with large black glasses stood from her seat and waved at them.

"That's my friend there. There are several seats. Join us?"

Her father turned quickly to her. "I don't know them," he hissed.

"It's family style. Come on." She guided him toward a seat where Mrs. C indicated. "Sit here."

Her father plopped down into the chair just as Nora was trying to push it in for him. He pulled himself forward, almost toppling her with him. The lady sitting at the table glared at her for a moment before breaking into a smile.

"This is my friend Helen." Mrs. Cipriani sat next to her friend.

"Nice to meet you, Mr. Harper." Helen offered him a sweet smile as she signaled a waiter.

"Ned." He scowled at the woman before turning to Nora. "I want to sit somewhere else."

"Dad, this is where we're sitting. We'll have our dinner soon."

Her father crossed his arms and slumped back against his chair, and she was reminded of little Katie throwing a temper tantrum.

Mrs. C poked her friend in the side, and the other woman gave up trying to wave down the waiter.

"She's trying to get them to give her wine." Mrs. Cipriani rolled her eyes.

"We can have alcohol if we want, Hazel. This is not a prison!" Her friend gave her a glare as she stood. "I'm going to track down that man and get us a glass." She turned to Nora. "Would your dad like some?"

"No, thank you."

Helen threw down her napkin and stomped away from the table.

"Don't worry. They don't serve alcohol here. She has a bit of what your father ails from," Mrs. Cipriani said.

"Do they all get grumpy?" Nora whispered.

Mrs. Cipriani shrugged. "I think it's because they can't remember, and that upsets them. They know something is wrong but ..." She stopped and tapped a finger to her temple.

"I see," Nora said.

Her father reached for his water glass, taking half the tablecloth with him and she grabbed his hand before he had upset the whole place setting. "Here, Dad. You're stuck."

"Damn thing." He turned to her with puppy dog eyes. "I can't seem to do anything right these days."

Nora patted his hand. He took a few sips and, sitting silently as he watched the comings and goings of other residents and staff.

"Mr. Harper, you did the funeral for my Sal. That was a few years ago now, but the service was lovely."

Nora's father sat up straighter as a smile came over his face. "Happy to help. Big Italian family, right?"

Mrs. Cipriani nodded. "Oh yes. Sal was the oldest of seven kids. Good Catholics, you know?" She winked at Nora's dad, and he laughed.

"Catholics certainly have interesting families. And long services."

"You don't have to tell me! Weddings and funerals can take all day. It's exhausting."

Helen came back with a scowl on her face. "No wine."

"Well, dear, I could have told you. But we can enjoy ourselves without alcohol."

Helen took a sip of her water and grimaced. "Would make the day more fun with it, though."

Mrs. Cipriani patted her friend on her shoulder. "Helen, did you know Ned here is a funeral director? He did my Sal's funeral a few years ago."

"Yep. Harper did my Harold's too." She nodded at Nora's father.

But he had gone back to fiddling with the silverware and Nora responded instead. "I hope we did our best for you and Harold."

"Fine, fine. No complaints." Helen turned again and waved to the waiter. When he stopped by, she said, "Any chance we could get some wine?"

Mrs. Cipriani reached for her friend's hand. "Helen, you have already asked." She leaned behind her friend and whispered to the waiter, "How about some grape juice in a fancy glass?"

He nodded, looking relieved, and fled from the table.

"There, see? He'll be right back."

Helen snapped her napkin to her lap. "About time we start getting what we pay for around here."

Mrs. Cipriani turned to Nora and sighed. "Tell me, dear, is your mother still with us?"

Nora glanced at her father who was engrossed in arranging the silverware. "No. She died a few years ago. It's just me, Dad, and my brother Dell and his family."

"Well at least that's something. Not married then?"

"Nope." Nora often resented the question, but realized it was warranted as she was well past "marrying age." Even though she bristled at the concept to think woman couldn't marry at any age in the present day.

But Mrs. Cipriani's friend surprised her by saying, "Better off if you ask me. Men these days don't treat women the way they should. My Harold treated me like a queen. Held the door for me. Bought me jewelry for every occasion. Served me wine every day." She glared at Mrs. C. "I sure do miss him."

"I'm sorry. Has he been gone long?" Nora asked the woman.

"Today is our anniversary." Helen wiped the corner of her eye with her napkin.

Hazel patted her friend's hand and whispered to Nora, "Ten years now. And it's not their anniversary. She thinks every day is, though."

The waiter brought a round of grape juice to the table in fancy glasses. When he set one down in front of Helen, she said, "Thank you, dear. Sorry to be a bother. Especially to such a fine-looking gentleman as yourself." She batted her nonexistent lashes at him, and he blushed.

Mrs. Cipriani winked at the boy. "Food next, please, before that goes to her head." He nodded, walking away once more.

The waiter began to bring food and her dad poked at his meat and potatoes with his fork. Nora smiled at her old art teacher. Today she was dressed in baggy pants covered in paint splotches. Her gray curls had been pulled back into a messy bun on top of her head, tendrils fallen to frame her wrinkled face.

"Are you keeping up with your art? You used to have some wonderful photography."

Nora felt herself blush as she shoved a bite of potato into her mouth. When she swallowed, she shook her head. "I did some small, odd jobs after college and took a trip to Paris. I loved being there and dreamed about going back, but things in life just twisted and turned until ... I'm helping run the funeral business now."

Mrs. C nodded as if she understood. "You don't have any interest in the photography anymore?"

"Oh no, I do. In fact, I was considering starting up a photography business too. Not sure I can juggle that plus Dad and the funeral home, though. Maybe photography is just something I should keep as a hobby."

"Do you take a lot of photographs ... as a hobby?"

Nora felt the warm rise in her cheeks again, knowing she'd not kept up with the photography in anyway until recently.

"Well, no. Things have been—"

Mrs. C held up her fork and smiled. "Keep up your creative endeavors, dear. The best way to get better is to keep at it."

Nora nodded. "I just took some photos for the Hoffmasters."

"Oh yes! They are a lovely family. Bud's granddaughter is taking care of him, yes?" Mrs. C raised her eyebrows at Nora.

"Yes, and she wanted some—" Nora looked at her father, not knowing how news about Bud might affect him. "Well, some photos of the whole family while Bud is still ... you know."

Mrs. C winked. "Yes, I understand. Did they turn out well? Did they like them?"

"Oh yes, his granddaughter Sarah really loves them, and I'm glad they'll have something to remember him by when he's gone."

"Do you think your purpose in your father's business—now your own—is to provide these pictures for your clients?"

"No." Nora shook her head. "I wasn't thinking that. I want to take family portraits, maybe newborns." Although she'd enjoyed taking pictures of the Hoffmasters, she wanted to celebrate life, not death.

Mrs. C nodded. "Sorry, I didn't mean to assume. But it'd be a good tie-in with the funeral home is all."

Nora sat back in her chair. The idea *did* tie in well. But no, she wanted to differentiate herself from the funeral home. Although ... could she do both?

Chapter Nineteen

Nora left the memory care center a little while later, after she'd settled her father back in his room. She thought about what Mrs. C had said as she drove to the funeral home. She needed to check out the second floor to see if her dad's idea of using that space would work.

She walked up the ornate staircase, forgoing the elevator they mainly used for moving boxes of stuff upstairs. Her hand trailed over the dark mahogany wood until she reached the top where a long hallway led to three closed doors. The air was colder up here—they kept the vents closed since the space was mostly unused—and she pulled her coat tighter around her. She walked to the first door and tried the knob. The door opened into a dark, square room with only one window allowing some light. Piles of boxes stood stacked almost to the low ceiling.

Maybe. But let's see what the other rooms look like.

She moved to the second door and pushed the door wide. A similar room greeted her with even more boxes.

I need to chat with Dell to see what is stored in these boxes.

She turned to the final door at the end of the hallway. Before opening it, she sent up a silent prayer.

Lord, if this is what you want, let me understand fully. Show me your path.

The door opened with a click and Nora gasped. The room was spacious with no boxes and a large bay window overlooking the back yard of the property. Above the window was a half oval, stained glass window that let in the sunlight in blues, reds, and purples. Instantly, her mind became filled with ideas.

I could bring up some of the Victorian furniture. That corner would be perfect for the tripod and some lighting. That stained glass might be a wonderful backdrop for some photos.

She moved to the small closet. Inside was just some old papers with a rod for hanging clothes. Perfect for storing some of her accessories.

Smiling, she turned and started back down the hallway.

Perfect! With a little paint and some cleanup, I could start using the room this month. I need to talk with Dell.

Nora bounded down the steps just as the front door swung wide.

"Nora!" Luke practically yelled across the short expanse.

She stepped down off the last step. "Luke, what are you doing here?"

Luke looked like he had been run over by a truck. Dark bags lined his bloodshot eyes. Had he been drinking or crying?

She hadn't known Luke for long, but she had never seen him anything but calm and peaceful. His shirt had come untucked from his pants on one side, and she noticed he had failed to button the shirt correctly, one side hung longer than the other.

As he stumbled forward toward her, she noticed the slight bit of stubble visible on his jaw. She slipped her hand into her pocket and wrapped her fingers around her cell.

Luke looked at her, then placed one hand on the railing to steady himself. "I was afraid you wouldn't be here."

"Would you like to come into my office?" She began making her way there. "I can make us some strong coffee."

"I'm not drunk, Nora," Luke said as he took a tentative step forward, wiping his face with both hands. He looked haggard now, Nora decided, tired. Caregiving was a hard business, she knew.

"Should I call Sarah?"

"We've been trying to call you. I think your phone might be off."

She took out her phone and realized, yes, she'd turned the thing off at the nursing home when the multiple pings had upset her father. She saw now that she'd missed several calls from Luke and Sarah.

When Luke looked up at her again, he appeared sad. Gone was the confident, gorgeous, professional businessman. A tired, worn-out shell stood in front of her.

"He's gone, Nora. Gone." A sob broke from Luke's throat, and she turned into his arms.

"I'm so sorry." Encircling his shoulders, she pulled him in tight. He hiccupped and sobbed some more. She hadn't realized Bud meant this much to Luke. She thought Sarah had been the one to truly feel the grief.

"Let's call your sister."

After talking with Sarah—her own sobs causing Nora to tear up—she called her brother. Luke sat sullenly in the chair opposite her desk, looking like a little child who'd lost his best friend while he waited.

"Okay, Luke, let's take your car back to the house. Dell is going to get some things here and meet us there."

Nora led Luke back to his car but settled herself behind the steering wheel. She wondered if her dad had ever had to do this before for a client.

Sarah met them at the front door a few minutes later. "Bud's gone."

Nora had to look away from the pained expression in Sarah's eyes. She watched instead as Luke slogged up onto the porch and through to the living room. She heard one of the kids crying.

"I know. You should tend to your family right now," she told Sarah. "Dell is coming right behind me. Let us do our job while you do yours."

Sarah put her head in her hands. For a moment, Nora let her grieve. Her father had always told them to go at the family's pace, to let them set the timing.

Finally, Sarah swiped away her tears and moved into the house. Nora followed.

Chapter Twenty

The next day, Nora made her way toward Ravensbridge to tell her father about Bud's passing. He would want to know about Bud, and she needed to see him, to be with her father as she worked on the grief that had settled in her chest. Yesterday had been a roller coaster of a day.

Last night, when Brian had steered their kids away to the kitchen, Dell and Nora had come in to do their duties. Nora had felt thankful for Dell's stoic and solid presence. His professional manner helped to calm her unease and settle her emotions. As they did their work, Nora noticed the care with which Dell took with each step of the process.

Afterward, she realized that being a mortician in a small town meant much more than simply dealing with the dead. You had to connect with the living too. And doing so might bring you additional grief. But she'd felt proud of the photos she'd taken a few weeks ago of the Hoffmasters. At least Sarah and her family, and even Nora and hers, could look back on those photos and smile.

Now, Dell would begin the embalming process as Nora worked with Sarah to set up the final details. Yet she needed to be with her father who had often comforted her. And to try to glean something from him. To learn how to deal with the emotional toll these deaths took on him. How had he done this for so many years? How had he watched family and friends pass away without breaking down into a sobbing mess.

She parked in Ravensbridge's parking lot and dug a tissue out of her purse to wipe her tear-streaked face. She didn't want to upset her father right off the bat. She needed to work up to telling him about Bud. Would he even remember his old friend? She didn't know, but she felt an obligation to tell him anyway.

She said hello to Susie again who said her father was in his room, waiting on lunch.

"You can accompany him to the dining hall if you wish," she told Nora.

When had Nora eaten last? She couldn't remember. Maybe right here at Ravensbridge yesterday.

She found her father pacing his room in an agitated state.

She put down her purse and lightly touched his arm. He turned angry eyes to her, and she flinched away from him, remembering how he had punched Dell not that long ago and how he had fought with Nurse John.

"Oh, Nora girl. Why ... what are you doing here?"

"I've come to take you to lunch. Are you ready?" She tried to plaster on her best smile. She didn't want to give him the news just yet but wanted to wait for a time when he was less agitated.

As she had the day before, she led her father to the dining hall where they were once again seated with Mrs. C and her friend.

"What a nice surprise!" Mrs. C exclaimed when she saw them. "Two days in a row."

Nora smiled and helped her father into his chair. When the waiter came with a burger and fries, he dug right in. Nora leaned over to Mrs. Cipriani.

"Bud Hoffmaster passed away last night. I want to tell Dad, but I'm not sure he will even know who I mean."

Mrs. Cipriani nodded. "That is a hard one. He might not need to know."

Nora thought about this for a moment before agreeing. "You're right. Telling him might just be to help me deal with the loss and not Dad." Nora poked at her own food. "I've grown to enjoy Bud's family—his granddaughter Sarah and her husband and children."

Nora needed to put on her funeral director's hat. She was no longer just a friend of the family. She needed to ensure Bud got the funeral he deserved. She glanced at her father again. He had pushed his plate away with barely a few bites eaten but was eyeing up the lemon meringue pie being passed around.

"Dad, I think you should eat a bit more of your lunch before dessert."

He turned to her, surprised. "Nora, when did you get here?"

She willed the tears welling up in her eyes to stop and said, "Just now, Dad. How about we split a piece of that pie?"

Mrs. C was right. Her father might not need to know. The reality would only cause too much pain and emotion he probably couldn't handle.

Chapter Twenty-one

Dell had been engrossed in his work when she arrived back at the funeral home later that day. When she had tried to chat, he had asked her to wait until he was finished. She agreed and retreated to her office.

Since she and Dell had cleared some of the bills and inventory issues, she set to work on the details of Bud's funeral instead. Some folks used a "neutral" place instead of the home, or sometimes their church provided the space. Bud hadn't wanted a church service, so they'd use the main parlor here at the funeral home, but Pastor Richfield would lead the service. They had some deliveries coming on Wednesday so she would try to avoid that day, but otherwise things were free. She checked Bud's file to ensure they had everything in stock that he had requested. The spreadsheets Dell had shown her the other day indicated they did have the necessary items. Once she spoke with Sarah, she could get the funeral cards printed and the obituary sent to the newspapers.

She pulled out the template for the obituary and noted the prices for each paper on a sticky note so she could advise Sarah. She'd make a copy of Bud's plans and put everything into a blue folder to take with her when she visited Sarah tomorrow.

Dell knocked on her office door. She waved him forward, and he sat in the chair across the desk from hers. The leather squeaked and a whoosh of air released from the seat as he sat. He held his hands in his lap, spine straight, slight scowl in place. He looked tired.

"Is everything okay?" she asked.

Dell sucked in a deep breath and pushed it out. "I'm fine. I just ... I just miss Dad. He and I always worked together when someone died. On the body, I mean." He leaned forward and put his forearms on the table.

Nora noticed a small tattoo on his left inner forearm. She squinted, trying to make out the design. She'd never seen this ink before, and Dell had never mentioned getting one.

"Not that I don't think you are working with me." He looked up at her. "Or at least trying."

"This isn't the first funeral you've done without Dad," Nora said.

"No, but every time just reminds me of what we've lost."

She thought about all the things she had lost due to her dad's illness. "I understand."

Dell wiped a hand over his face. "Of course you do. He's your dad too." The eyes he looked at her with now were sad, almost sheepish. "Sorry."

"Don't be. We're all dealing in our own way." She waited a beat, letting Dell have his moment. "I wanted to talk to you about the stuff on the second floor."

Dell frowned. "It's just some extra things. Although, I haven't been up there in a while. We should probably go through it."

She nodded. "We can. But the room at the back is empty. I was thinking I could use that as my studio."

Dell sighed. "You're still going to do that? I really need you here. To help run this business."

"But don't you see? I would be here. It's perfect. I can grow my photography business while still helping you. I'll just clean up that room a bit. It'll be great."

"I don't know, Nora. Can we talk about this later?"

Although she really wanted her brother's approval, she could tell he was feeling emotional. Now was not the time. She stood and said, "Let's go home. It's been a long day and I bet the kids miss you."

Dell smiled up at her. "Natalie was making some coffee cake. Want some?"

At Dell's, the siblings sat hunched over cups of coffee while the kids began cleaning up their coloring supplies that were strewn on the kitchen table. Natalie pulled a coffee cake from the fridge. After slicing the dessert into pieces, she pulled paper plates and forks from the cupboard and began serving. The kids yelled their happiness and took their seats around the table dutifully.

Nora wished she had her camera with her to capture these moments. Although they weren't what most people deemed "special," she never wanted to forget a single moment of her life with these loved ones. She never wanted to worry about remembering them the way her father did.

When Natalie set down a large piece of coffee cake, Nora waved her off. "I had pie earlier with Dad."

"This doesn't have any calories, especially during hard days," Natalie told her with a wink. She slid the piece in front of Nora before sitting back down.

Dell looked at the smaller piece his wife had handed him before raising his eyes to his sister.

Nora swiftly shifted her piece to Dell as he pushed his plate her way. When Natalie started to interrupt, Nora said, "No calories, right?"

Natalie sighed and picked up her own fork. "Okay. But just for tonight."

Dell kissed her cheek before digging into his cake.

When the kids began to squabble over which one of them had the biggest slice, Natalie interjected. "Mason, Ethan, Brett, take your sister into the other room and eat your cake. No arguing." She pointed one finger at them and raised her eyebrows. "If you argue, I'll come take away the cakes and the TV *and* your video games." Ethan's eyes grew wide at this threat. "Mason, be sure the little ones don't spill any."

The children rose carefully from the table and made their way into the living room. Once again, Nora longed for her camera. She'd need to start carrying her equipment more.

"And be nice!" Natalie called just as Brett shoved Ethan, nearly knocking his cake from his hands. She turned to Nora and said, "Sure you don't want to take at least one home with you? For, say, a month or so?"

Nora laughed. "Nope. I'm just the aunt, remember. Sugar them up, go home is my motto." She took a bite of her cake, chewed, and put down her fork. She really wasn't hungry. She wanted to talk about their father, her business ... their future. "Does Dad know you when you visit?" she asked her brother.

Dell shrugged. "Sometimes. But he often thinks I'm still a kid."

Nora knew all about that and told him so. "But there are moments of lucidity. And even some moments that aren't in the present but still bring back good memories." Nora thought of the rope swing she and her dad had talked about.

And how her heart felt when he talked to her as if she was a little girl. The girl he loved unconditionally.

"I wish Dad had more lucid moments," she told her brother. "I just feel like he should know about Bud."

"Maybe tomorrow will be a better day for him? He does still have moments when things are clear."

Nora pushed the cake on her plate around with her fork. "I don't know, Dell. He's been really off since we put him there."

"Don't say it like that." Dell put down his fork with a clatter and frowned. "You know I had to make this choice. Things here were—"

Nora put up a hand to stop him. "I don't blame you. I just wish things weren't like this."

Her brother nodded, picking up his fork again. "Me too."

"He did have some clear moments today." She speared another piece of cake and put the chunk into her mouth, but she had no desire to eat more and put down the fork once more. "I wish Mom were here. She would know how to handle him."

"You can't say for sure," Dell said as he pressed his finger onto the last crumbs from his plate. "This all came on after she died. And she was always kind of focused on herself."

Dell was right. Their mother had been a good woman, a good wife, and a decent mom, but she had often thought more of herself than she did others. Many times, Dell and Nora had to fix their own meals when their dad had been late at the funeral home. Their mother had often sequestered herself away in her room when their father was busy or late getting home, claiming he didn't love her enough to come home on time. Even though she knew the demands of the funeral home. People didn't die between the hours of nine and five.

"But she knew Dad," Nora said now. "I bet she would know what to say to bring him back to the present. Or give him clarity." She sat back in her chair. "It's hard to even understand this disease. He mostly remembers me, but I'm not always an adult in his eyes. How about you?"

Dell raised his eyebrows at Natalie as he reached for another piece. When she moved the cake out of range, he rose to put his plate and fork in the dishwasher. "I'm usually a child to him. Almost never a man. He still bosses me around, telling me to cut the lawn or shovel the sidewalk." Her brother sank back into his chair.

"I think maybe you guys should see a counselor," suggested Natalie.

"What kind of counselor?" Dell asked.

"A grief counselor maybe." Natalie rose to clean up the remaining plates and put the cake away.

"But Dad is still alive," Nora said.

"But grief isn't just about death." Natalie sat back down and folded her hands on the table. "It happens whenever we lose something. You've lost your mother and now your father, really. Or maybe you just need to talk to someone who knows more about dementia."

Nora thought the idea might have some merit. "But I don't know where we would find someone like that."

"Isn't Sarah's husband some kind of counselor?" Dell asked.

Nora felt dumb for not knowing after all the time she had spent with Sarah's family. But she hadn't talked with Brian much, only little things like telling him where to stand for pictures.

"I'll have to ask, I guess. I really don't know." Nora thought about his question for a moment. Dad fluctuated in and out of his present state of mind at any given time.

She hadn't noticed a better or worse part of the day. "I'm not sure," she said. "I'm not sure there is ever a perfect time for his memory. Although he does love talking about the business."

She thought of how her father had lit up when talking with Mrs. Cipriani and Helen.

Dell scratched at a spot on his jeans. "What do you talk about with him?"

"I let him lead, usually. The doctors tell us not to try to argue with him, but to just let his own thoughts play out. It's better not to frustrate him."

"I know all that, but I just get frustrated when he scolds me like I'm a child." Dell kept scratching at his pants leg until Nora wondered if he might wear a hole in the denim. "Maybe we could go together sometime?"

"Sure. And what about the kids and Natalie?"

Dell exchanged a look with his wife. "Natalie doesn't think we should take the younger kids, and she can't go with me if we don't." He glanced at her again before saying, "Maybe that's what makes this all harder. I really could use her support when I'm there."

Natalie squeezed his hand. "I want to go, babe. I just don't know what to do about the kids."

Dell nodded. Nora felt a bit of emptiness inside. Jake had never really been there for her in these kinds of things. Would she ever find someone who she could truly share life with?

She pushed those thoughts from her mind for now. She needed to focus on her dad, her family, and the business. Love, if it happened, would have to come later. She wanted to give her brother the support he needed, especially since she'd left him in the lurch weeks ago to relax at the beach.

"Let's go visit Dad together tomorrow, okay?"

Dell perked up. "Early? I really think he's better in the morning."

Nora agreed, hoping for her brother's sake that their father would be coherent.

She rose to leave, and her brother asked, "Do you have everything situated for Bud's memorial?"

She nodded. "Yes. We had almost everything set up before Bud died. Sarah picked next Saturday for the funeral so her mom and people from out of town could attend. They have a large family, I guess."

She hugged Natalie and kissed her brother on the cheek. "Thanks for being here. Not sure what I would do without my family."

"Same," Dell said, rising to give her a fierce hug. "We're going to get through this." He looked into her eyes, and she nodded.

In the living room, the three boys had finished their cake, and Katie was now playing with a doll, her cake sitting mostly untouched.

"You didn't want your cake, Katie?" she asked the little girl.

She shrugged but concentrated on her doll.

"Well, if you want that piece, you better eat it before your brothers do."

Brett reached out and tried to swipe her dessert. Katie squeaked, snatching the plate away. She rose, dolly under her arm, and stomped off to the kitchen. Nora heard Natalie soothe her little girl then call to the boys, "If the rest of you are done, bring those plates back in here."

Brett and Mason hopped up immediately, but Ethan stayed glued to his game. Nora sat next to him for a moment, watching as the duck on the screen ate gems and racked up points.

"Looks fun," she said.

Ethan shrugged, never taking his eyes off the game. "Pop Pop used to love this game and always tried to beat me at the high score." Ethan looked up at her. "Can you tell Pop Pop he should come home soon so we can play again? He always gave the best piggyback rides too."

You're not wrong, kid.

She kissed the top of Ethan's head and said, "I'll do my best, little man."

She would have to mention to Dell and Natalie that the kids needed to see their grandfather. She knew they were trying to keep the hard facts of his illness from their innocent lives, but they needed to see him.

She rose again, determined to keep moving forward.

Chapter Twenty-Two

Dell met her early the next day outside Ravensbridge. She took note of his crisply ironed shirt and sharp slacks.

"What's with the fancy dress clothes?"

Dell pulled at the collar. "I thought maybe if Dad saw me in business clothes, he'd see me as a grown man."

The day was brisk, and Nora pulled her coat closer around her neck. October was already halfway over. Dell's kids would soon be picking out Halloween costumes, and Natalie would be planning Thanksgiving before long. Nora wondered how they should include their father this year. Would it be better to come to the home to visit and bring food or take him from the facility for the day?

Dell stamped his feet as he waited for her. "Winter's coming quick."

"Yep. Let's get inside."

She hadn't slept well all night, worrying about this meeting. Would her dad see them as they were now—grown adults? Would he remember one sibling, but forget the other? How would his reaction hurt either of them?

Some days she felt like life would be easier to just let their father alone, to not visit at all. How could they deal with his worsening dementia? The reality of the disease felt like a death while he still lived, trapped inside his aging body.

The door swished open, and Nora strode toward the desk to check in. Susie once again greeted her from her perch behind the desk.

"Hello, Nora. I thought today was Dell's day."

Nora smiled as she signed herself and Dell in on the sheet. "It is, but we thought we'd both visit together today. Maybe he'd have more of a connection."

Susie smiled but didn't offer any encouragement.

She's probably seen enough to know we're delusional.

Nora put down the pen and said, "See you later."

As they walked through the double doors and into the main hallway, Dell said, "Kind of like a prison, isn't it?"

"I think that myself almost every time I come here."

Dell had initially disagreed with her assessment, saying the doubly locked doors added good security to keep the residents safe and where the staff could properly care for them. And while Nora did understand that bit, the place still felt like a prison. She was glad he could see both sides of the argument now.

Nora and Dell walked down the hallway toward their father's room, but she spotted him in the games room before they had gone too far. She veered into the games room, hoping not to have to break up another fight between her father and the staff.

But this time her father was all smiles as he played a card game with Mrs. Cipriani, Helen, and another woman Nora hadn't met. Nora smiled as she walked up to their table.

"Hey, who's winning?" Nora looked down at the table where chips lay scattered around between the players. "Wait. Are you playing poker?"

"Nora!" Her father glanced at her briefly before once again scrutinizing his cards. "Grab a seat and give us a minute. Dell! Glad to see you too. What a nice surprise to have you both here. Pull up a chair."

"It's too late to deal them in!" Helen spat from her side of the table, holding her cards close to her chest.

"Calm down, Helen," Mrs. Cipriani said, "They're just watching." She whispered, "Don't worry, no real cash at stake here. We play for pudding cups or ice cream."

Nora sat back against the chair Dell had pulled up for her and smiled. "Oh good."

"Shush!" Helen scolded again. "Ned needs to play."

"What will it be, Ned?" Mrs. C asked.

"I'll call." Her father threw two chips into the pile.

Mrs. C did the same. The fourth player did the same and the group revealed their cards.

"Shoot!" cried the unknown woman.

"Now, Florence, don't be a sore loser." Helen drew the chips her way and smiled.

"You would say that, since you've won almost every hand." Florence pushed away from the table. "I'm done for today. If I bet anymore, I won't have dessert for a week."

Ned laughed as he turned to Nora and Dell.

"Good to see you, Son." He offered him his hand in greeting and Dell reached out, all smiles.

"Hey, Dad."

"Well, it's a fine day to come out. Sorry you had to see me lose to a bunch of women."

Helen stacked her chips and grunted. "You won a couple of hands by the looks of your stacks."

Mrs. C gathered up her chips and said, "We all did decently except Florence." She looked over her shoulder to make sure the other woman had walked away. "She doesn't know when to quit." She turned to Helen and said, "Let's go, dear." Mrs. C winked at Nora as the duo shuffled away.

Nora laughed, and the feeling felt good in her chest. She hadn't seen her dad this lucid or happy in a long time. Maybe Dell was right about the morning hours being the best for him. She finally felt like maybe the move here was a good thing.

"How's the business, Dell?" her father asked, leaning back in his chair.

"Good. I've been catching Nora up on some stuff and figuring out all you did on a daily basis. I think we have a handle on things now."

"She's a quick learner." Her dad winked in her direction, and she smiled.

"We'll have our first run together at Bud Hoffmaster's funeral next week and—"

Her father sat upright in his chair, and Nora cringed.

"Bud died?"

She could swat her brother right now.

"Dad, I meant to tell you but hadn't gotten the chance. Bud passed away a few days ago."

Her father frowned for a moment before saying, "We were just talking about hitching a ride out of town together."

Dell and Nora remained quiet for a moment, letting her father process the information and work through the disconnect in his brain. Nora prayed silently that the news wouldn't send him into a tailspin.

After a few moments of silence, Nora said, "Bud told me about your trip to New York state all those years ago." She prayed this statement wouldn't make things worse. "Said you wanted to run away."

Her father snorted. "Yep. Didn't want to be a mortician. Thought I could make it big somewhere else. I almost did too. Until we ran out of money." Her father frowned, and Nora prayed again that the memory would hold. "I should call Bud."

Dell opened his mouth, but Nora put her hand on his. "Dad. Bud passed away. We're doing his funeral on Saturday."

Once again, her father frowned, but nodded. "You found his file?"

She nodded. "Yep. And I was able to go over things with him and his granddaughter prior, so everything is set. He was a much-loved man."

Her father gazed off at a group of women staring at a morning talk show on the TV. "Yes ... yes, he was."

Nora saw a dark look pass over her father's face as he slapped his hand against his thigh. "Let's go have a drink to Ned!"

Dell looked at Nora. "Uh ... Dad, I don't think—"

"Dad, I don't think they allow alcohol in here."

"So let's go out. We must honor my friend, Nora. I think he might be the last I have left."

Nora considered the implications of moving her dad from the home. Although, doing so was not against the rules, going outside the security of the facility was discouraged for dementia patients who could become a handful once outside the home's doors. But they could take one car, and she had Dell with her in case things got dicey.

She looked at her brother and whispered, "What do you think?"

"I guess it'd be okay. There's two of us to his one. And he seems really with it—"

"Will you two quit whispering like I'm not here," their father interrupted.

Nora cringed as she realized the time. "It's a bit early for a drink, Dad."

"It's almost noon," their father said. "That little bar about a block from the funeral home offers some pub grub. We can grab a bite and a drink. To Bud."

Nora glanced at her brother who was already standing. "Okay, Dad."

After signing her father out and promising to have him back before sun went down, the trio stepped outside and began walking to Nora's car.

Her father stopped and took a deep breath. "Ah, smell that freedom."

"Dad, you can go outside." The courtyard felt like a lovely place to Nora when they had sat there.

Her dad frowned at her. "The walls are confining in there. And the wallpaper is plain ugly. Don't know why I let your mother talk me into that pattern." He took another deep breath in. "I could eat some French fries!"

Chapter Twenty-three

Nora and her dad sat at a small table inside Lucky's Lounge, one of the only bars in Millsburgh, while Dell went to grab them a few drinks. Nora hadn't been inside the place in many years, perhaps back to her twenty-first birthday when Jill had dragged her here for her first drink. The floor stuck to her shoes, and she wondered if the linoleum had been cleaned in all that time. She kept herself from leaning on the table, unsure what mystery stickiness might linger there.

She had never been inside a bar with her father, and she wasn't sure how to conduct herself. Would he snap into a different mode any minute and wonder why his twelve-year-old daughter was in a bar? Would he even remember who she was?

But her father smiled wider than she had seen in a long time as he tipped back his chair onto two legs. She fought the urge to scold him. If he fell, there might be broken bones involved. But she kept silent as he looked to be enjoying himself for the first time in ages. She was happy he wasn't being his normally grumpy self. He watched a news program being broadcast on a TV above the bar, taking in the show with interest.

Dell came back with two beers and a coffee for Nora.

"Sure you don't want to join us, punkin?" her dad said before slurping off the foam from the top of his beer.

"DD," she said, raising her coffee cup in salute. "Someone has to drive."

"To old friends," Dell said, holding up his beer mug.

"Who are you callin' old?" her father joked. "To Bud." He clinked his mug against Dell's.

The men took sips and sighed as men do while Nora warmed her hands against the coffee mug. The brew was bitter, but hot, and she felt the last bit of tension release from her shoulders.

Although this was not a scenario she was used to with her father, she was glad for a bit of normalcy in their lives.

The men talked about the business, and she tried to keep track, but soon talk of accounting and audits dulled her senses. She marveled at her father's lucidity. Would they ever understand this disease? The constant worry about what he'd remember put her off kilter. Talking with him felt like a whole new language to her.

She liked the way Dell laughed with their dad and the easy way the men had with one another. Maybe he remembered Dell more than her?

Dad slapped Dell's back, making him half spill his beer. "Bud, you're a hoot!"

Dell stiffened, but she shook her head and he just smiled, letting the moment pass.

She sipped her coffee as if she sat in the best coffeehouse in town, determined to enjoy this bit of peace.

When she had finished her coffee, she stood to get another at the bar. The place was practically deserted at this time of day, but she still had to wait for the bartender who had disappeared somewhere in the back. She looked in the mirror behind the bar at her dad and Dell conversing. She was glad Dell could keep the conversation going despite a few missteps from their father. When the bartender finally came out, wiping his hands on a towel, he refilled her cup and told her the drink was on the other man's tab.

She smiled, loving how Dell took care of those he loved. He'd always been a great older brother. She hoped she'd be able to foster an even stronger relationship with him as they moved forward in keeping the business afloat together.

She turned back to their table with her coffee mug in hand, but stopped short when she noticed only Dell now sitting at the table.

She strode to his side. "Where's Dad?"

Dell swallowed a gulp of beer. "Bathroom."

Nora looked down the dark hallway to where the bathrooms were. "By himself?"

"He seemed fine, Nor, and I haven't gone to the bathroom with my dad since I could barely hold my own ... you know." Dell winked before taking another sip of his beer.

A tight knot of tension began to build in Nora's gut. *What if he forgot where he was? What if someone distracted him?*

But no, there was no one around and the path to the bathrooms was clear. She could see the door from here. She sat down, never taking her eyes from the bathroom area.

How long did she talk with the bartender after watching them in the mirror? How long did it take an elderly man to go to the bathroom?

"How long has he been gone?" she asked.

"Only a few minutes. I'm sure he'll be fine, Nor," Dell said, picking up on her tension. "He goes to the bathroom on his own at the home."

Nora nodded, but kept her eyes fixed on the hallway as she sat. "But he gets confused easily. And we're not at the home. This isn't even a place he's that familiar with."

SUE A. FAIRCHILD

"He appeared lucid today."

Dell went back to the bar to grab two more beers, while Nora continued to stare at the bathroom door. She looked down briefly to consult the time on her phone. When her brother returned to the table, she looked again. Five minutes had passed and the knot in Nora's stomach grew. Dell, too, now seemed to begin to feel her unease as he remained quiet and barely touched his beer.

At the ten-minute mark, Nora told him, "Go in there and see what's wrong."

Dell rose without a word and strode to the bathroom. He was gone for only a few seconds, but when he came out from the room, he shook his head slightly.

Their father was gone.

Chapter Twenty-four

Nora had first checked the room herself, then went to talk to the bartender while Dell checked the outside of the bar. No one had seen her dad walk off, mainly because there was not anyone there to see anything. The bartender had been helping her or had been in the kitchen. Dell hadn't kept his eyes trained on the door when Nora's dad had excused himself to go to the bathroom. Their dad could be just about anywhere by now.

She had shouted at Dell before stomping over to talk with the bartender. So much for building a better, stronger relationship.

But how could he have taken his eyes off him for even a second?

Lord, help us find him. And keep us from killing each other in the process.

She noticed the time on her phone. Another fifteen minutes had passed.

Dell had called the authorities, and as Nora walked outside, a black Dodge charger pulled up. A tall police officer got out. He walked toward her with his hand on his hip.

"Mr. Dell Harper?" he asked.

"Yes. This is my sister Nora."

"Your dad has gone missing?"

She nodded and the officer took out a notepad and pencil. Nora proceeded to tell him about her father, about his dementia, and answered several other questions he had while Dell stood mutely by.

"Normally we wait twenty-four hours before anyone is missing," the officer told them.

"But our father has dementia," Nora pleaded. "He just didn't go somewhere else on his own. He can't be on his own. He's obviously confused."

Her brother's face was a stormy sea. His eyes red and wild. She was not sure his appearance indicated grief or anger. He ran a hand through his already disheveled brown hair. *Oh, how he looks like Dad*. Why had she never noticed before?

"Did he appear confused when he went to the bathroom?" the officer asked.

Nora looked at her brother. The men had been in a normal conversation when she'd left the table to get her coffee. "Did Dad seem off at all when he left the table?"

"Well ..." Dell shuffled his feet, kicking a stone across the parking lot. "He said he had to go to the bathroom. Although ..." Her brother looked up at Nora with the look of a child caught in the act.

"*What*?"

"He said something about draining the fluid out of a body, but I thought he was making a joke about ... you know ... peeing."

Nora squatted down in the parking lot with her face in her hands and began to sob.

Dell talked with the officer for a moment, emphasizing the dementia aspect.

"I don't think they wait twenty-four hours when it's a dementia patient," he told the officer who agreed to go check with his superiors.

When the officer walked back to his car, Dell bent down next to Nora and rubbed her back. "It's going to be okay."

She lashed out at him. "You don't know that! He could be anywhere. Hurt. Bleeding. Definitely confused." *Oh, why did we take him out of the home?*

Dell stood again as the officer approached. Nora stood as well, her tears spent and her rage rising.

"We'll begin looking right away," the officer told them. "A call has gone out with a description of your father. If you can get us a photo, that would be better."

Good. She needed to *do something.* She took out her phone and showed the officer a recent pic of her father. He asked her to text the photo to him and she did. But now her part was done as he went to send the image to other searchers.

She couldn't just sit around and wait on others.

"Dell, get in the car." She strode toward her vehicle as she dug her keys out of her purse. She heard her brother say something additional to the officer before trotting up beside her.

"Where are we going?" he asked.

"I don't know, but I can't just sit here." She called back to the officer, "You have my number, please keep me posted and I'll do the same."

He tipped his hat in acknowledgement, then walked back to his own car.

Chapter Twenty-five

"Nora, it's going to be okay," Dell said as she made her way slowly down every side street in Millsburgh. His hand touched her shoulder, and she flinched. He turned back to the passenger window and fell silent.

She felt cold and turned up the heater. Dad would be cold too, she thought, out in the elements. A smattering of rain began to hit the windshield and she gritted her teeth.

Why did this have to happen? Couldn't anything ever go right? Hadn't she tried to do all the right things? *Why God?*

She felt as if caught between opposing forces—the need to do the right thing and the desire to chuck everything and run. She shook her head of the thoughts. This was not some movie scene. This was real life. She was not being pulled in any direction, and she wouldn't run. They just needed to find their father.

Help, Lord.

She touched Dell's knee with her hand and felt him flinch this time. "I know. I'm just scared."

"I should have protected him. What were we thinking, taking him out ..." Dell looked out at the passing colorful trees. "I wanted him to treat me like a man, an adult, but as soon as he seemed like Dad again, I acted like a child."

"Dell, it's not your fault. We're both trying to figure this out, and Dad was very lucid today." Nora glanced at him then back at the road. "Dad wanted to remember his friend, and we wanted to feel normal again."

Dell shoved his hand through his hair, grunted, and shifted in his seat. "We should go back for my car so I can look in different places. And let the home know."

Nora nodded as she swung the wheel around toward the facility. "You're right. We need more eyes on this."

"Any ideas on where he might go?"

"Back to the center maybe? Maybe he's already there waiting," she suggested.

She knew that was simply wishful thinking. They'd been several miles from the home, and her father would never have been able to walk that far in this amount of time. Plus, he didn't even want to be there.

We should have never put him there.

Dell grunted. "Doubtful. He doesn't really like living there. I should have never put him in there in the first place."

Nora began to agree but fought back the urge to keep blaming her brother. "That's not fair, Dell. We made the decision together, and your family needed it. He just needed time to adjust, and his loss of memory made doing so harder."

Dell grunted again as she pulled into Ravensbridge's parking lot. She knew she needed to think of something. She needed Dell's head in this search. She knew once her brother had a task to accomplish, his emotions would fade away like a bad memory.

"You're right. He wouldn't go back to the nursing home. He keeps wanting to get out. But we should go in and check."

Dell agreed and went in to check while she waited in the car. Nora thought about the places that meant the most to her father. When Dell returned to the car with a grim look she said, "Maybe his own home?"

Dell nodded. "I could see that. Or maybe my house?" Dell's eyebrows raised. "Natalie and the kids are alone. What if—"

"He won't hurt them, Dell. We have to believe that. But give them a quick call to be on the lookout."

Dell took out his phone and called Natalie, outlining everything that had happened. "No, don't bring the kids out. I don't want to upset them," he said into the phone. "I'll call you when we know more or find him. Just pray. And call Pastor Richfield and start the prayer chain."

When he clicked to end the call, he turned back to Nora.

"No sign of him at home either. Natalie can see Dad's house from ours too, so she'll keep an eye out. I asked her to keep the kids busy so they don't sense anything wrong."

"Good idea," Nora agreed as Dell moved toward his own car. "Maybe Mom's grave?" she called to him.

Her father hadn't visited the site often, preferring to talk to the photo of his wife from their wedding day. He had always said, "I can't talk to a hunk of stone. I need to see her face."

Had they moved that picture with him to the home? Nora tried to envision his room and where the framed photo might set. There were not many places, and she thought the nightstand would have been the place so he could see the picture every day.

"Where is that picture of Mom from their wedding day?" she asked her brother. "The one with just her and taken outside somewhere."

"The old oak," Dell answered, his hand on his car's door handle. "She told me they had taken the photo before she got in the car to go meet Dad at the church."

Nora nodded. She remembered the story too. And now felt even guiltier for having taken down the tree.

"But where is it? We didn't move it to the home, right? I don't remember the picture being at the house."

"I don't remember moving it either. He had so few things to take along, I would have remembered that. But I haven't seen the photo lately," Dell said, rubbing his chin.

Nora looked out through the windshield. "Okay. I'll drive by the cemetery and check."

Dell agreed. "I'll run over to his house to check. If I think of anywhere else I'll call you."

She pulled out from the parking lot and toward the cemetery.

Where are you, Dad? Lord, please help.

Nora pulled away from her mother's grave about fifteen minutes later with something nagging at her. She'd gotten out and visited the grave for a few minutes—it hadn't felt right to not get out and pay her respects. But as she stood over the spot, thinking of her mother, something had stirred in her brain, but she couldn't pinpoint what.

"Lord, I know you're trying to tell me something. I can feel that small voice you use to direct me. But I need whatever you're telling me to be clearer."

Praying out loud to God felt odd. She'd been lapse in her studies and prayer with him lately. What had kept her away? Oh, right. Jake. Her trip to the Outer Banks. Dad moving into the home. Dealing with the business.

I am with you always.

God wasn't someone to just spend time with when things weren't going well. She knew cultivating a relationship with him would help in every aspect of her life. Yet, she'd been trying to figure things out on her own.

"Sorry, Lord. I promise to do better. And I really need your help now. I know you're with Dad too right now, but I need to be with him to be sure he's okay. Please lead me to him."

She turned down another side street and saw a man walking. Her heart beat faster for a moment until she realized the man wasn't her father, just some older fellow with a cane.

She turned down another street and thought about Bud. Would he know where Dad might go if he were still here? Maybe she should call Sarah. No. She was dealing with her own grief right now.

She thought about her mother again, wondering how she and her father had met. Why had she never asked for that story? She'd not asked her father enough about his life, she realized now. And now it might be too late.

She thought about that photo again of her mother on her wedding day in front of the big oak. Where could that be? She scanned another alleyway and moved slowly on, squinting to see inside storefronts. Maybe he'd gone shopping? She shook her head. Dad hated shopping. She thought about what the aide had told her, about how Alzheimer's patients were ruled by their emotions. What was Dad passionate about? What did he care most about?

The funeral home.

Nora slammed on the brakes causing the person in the car behind her to honk their horn. She waved out the window, then pulled over and called Dell.

Chapter Twenty-six

When Nora arrived back at the funeral home, the building was dark. She thought for a moment about waiting for Dell, but she just had to see if Dad was inside. She used her key to enter the business, clicked on the hall light, strode right to her dad's ... *her* office ... and swung open the door.

The light from the hallway glinted off something and she clicked the switch to turn on more light. There on her desk sat the photo of her mother on her wedding day in a silver frame.

She plopped down into the guest chair, feeling frustrated. She picked up the photo and touched the image of her mother's face. She remembered now. She'd moved the picture here to the office, thinking Dad wouldn't even miss it.

As Nora sat alone in her father's office, she could hear only the ticking of the grandfather wall clock in the corner. A gift from one of Dad's relatives when they had served overseas in the military. The ticking came slower now, and she realized she hadn't wound the timepiece in a few days. She checked the hour on her phone. The clock was significantly behind. She rose to remedy the problem, moving the hour hand ahead. The clock struck the time as Nora closed the lid and let the sound wash over her. The clock and its chimes had been a constant in the funeral home since she was little and always brought a bit of comfort to her soul.

Yet now she still felt uneasy. Where had he gone? How could they find him? She had been so sure he would have come here. To talk to Mom. She remembered how they had often chatted with her in the office. "To be away from you kids," Mom had once told her. They'd been told not to play in the front rooms of the funeral home and had always had a playroom toward the back.

The clock chimed its last note, and she looked up at it, remembering better times.

"I always loved that clock."

Nora spun around with wide eyes. "Dad!"

Her father looked spent, as if he had walked across a desert to get here.

Nora practically ran to him in what little space the office provided.

"We were so worried about you." She clung to her father as tears rolled down her face. But she pulled back when she realized her father didn't reciprocate the hug. His eyes had a distant look to them as he surveyed the office behind her.

"You haven't changed anything."

She let go of him and turned to see what he saw. The 1970s-style filing cabinets in avocado green, a large mahogany desk with an ancient computer including a floppy disk section and her laptop, which almost looked out of place with the other items surrounding it.

"I haven't ... well, I haven't had time or—"

"You need to make this place your own."

Her father moved around the desk, his fingers trailing over the dark wood desktop. He stood behind the desk for a minute before pulling the desk chair closer and sitting. The leather squeaked, and Nora felt a flash of memory when she had come in to ask her dad something at the age of fourteen, but he was sitting at his desk as he was now, head in his hands. She had backed out of the office without saying anything, feeling the need to respect his privacy. Later, she had learned her paternal grandmother had died. Dad and Gram Harper had been close. He had done her service a week later with nary a tear in his eye, but Nora knew he had grieved in private that day behind his desk.

Nora looked around the office as she moved quietly forward to the chair Dell had occupied only a few days earlier. She hoped he would get here soon. She should call him again, but she felt a sense of ... something that made her sit and remain quiet in her father's presence.

After a few moments, her father wiped his hands over his face and looked at her. He smiled, but the light didn't reach his eyes like it once did. She smiled back, waiting for him to make the first move.

He sighed and picked up the photo in the frame on his desk.

"I used to sit here every day and pray for the people of this town. For the folks I might know that walked in that door next, grieving their loved one. For my family." He gazed at the photo in his hands for a while, kissed the glass, and put the frame back down on the desk. "Now, I pray for God to help me retain names and relationships." He put his head in his hands again. "I can't even remember my kids sometimes."

The last bit had been softer, almost spoken as a whisper, but Nora had heard. And the confession ripped at her heart. He would be gone to them soon, and she thought she was the only one who had noticed. But Dad knew what he would be losing too. He was mourning all the information he could never pass along to her just as she had been mourning what she'd never learned.

"I'll have to cultivate my own relationships, Dad. Work on knowing people the way you did. I'm sure you didn't know everything when you first took over the business from Grandpa."

He shook his head and wiped tears from his eyes. "I'm sorry. I should have done better. I thought … forgive me … I thought …"

Lights flashed through the front window and a car door slammed. Nora heard the front door open, then the whisper of feet on the plush carpet behind her. She turned slightly to see her brother.

"Dad," he said, tentatively. "I'm so glad you're here."

Nora silently praised her brother for keeping his cool and speaking calmly. She knew his heart must be beating just as wildly as her own.

"Son, come sit." Her father motioned to the other chair.

Nora smiled as the seat did its little *whoosh* thing as her brother sat. She watched him fidget for a moment before turning her attention back to her father. A realization hit her, and she felt a surge of hope.

"Dad and I have been talking about relationships. How he used to … how he prays for people. The ones who have to use our services."

Dell cleared his throat and fidgeted again in his chair. She turned to him.

"Dad was talking about how he bonded with the clients. Knew them. Knew their families." Dell nodded and she continued, "How he's afraid that will get lost now that he can't remember."

"Nora has your knack, Dad. For caring. Did you know she's started taking photos? Bud's family hired her to take some before he died. Precious images they'll have forever now because of her."

Her father turned to him with raised eyebrows. "What?"

Dell rubbed his hands over his pants, opened his mouth to speak, but then closed it. Tried again. "She's going to set up a studio upstairs. An extra service for our clients." He looked at Nora and she smiled.

Their father nodded and looked back out the window. "I don't belong here anymore. You two are doing fine without me."

Nora's heart broke for her father. All the years he had put into this business for their family, for the people of this town, and she had only seen the … ickiness of owning a funeral home. But the business had been all about caring, really. Helping people grieve. She felt sick now. How rash and ugly she had been to try to run away from it.

Their father turned back toward them and said, "Bud's dead?"

Nora glanced at Dell, who winced. "Yes, I'm sorry."

Their father's disease reared its head again. They had discussed Bud's death earlier. The moment had been the whole reason they had left the home—to drink a toast to Bud. But her father had obviously forgotten. *Oh, what it must be like to have grief refreshed in that way.*

Her father nodded. "You told me before, right?" She nodded, and he looked down at his hands. "He told you we tried to run away?"

"Yes, when I first went to see him and finalize his paperwork."

"We didn't *try*, we *did*. We got as far as the New York state border before we realized we had nowhere to go and very little money to get there. And I missed my mama. And your mama—that was before she would give me the time of day, though. I wanted to prove to her I had a purpose of my own, but I had no other talents." Her father barked out a short laugh. "My lack of skills, this town, and its people drew me back quicker than a yo-yo at the end of a very short string."

Nora sat in silence for a moment. He'd not spoken this much in so long. "Do you regret staying?" Nora asked.

"Nope." The quick answer surprised her. "Not for one minute. I dug into the work when we returned. Shadowed my father every second of the day—pert near drove him mad." He smiled and looked at Dell. "Dad was even less of a communicator than I was, but to the public? The clients? Caring, sweet, merciful, attentive ..."

He reached across the desk with his hand, and Nora grasped onto it tightly. "I just wish we could do this together like I did with my dad."

"We can try."

Her father released her hand and shook his head. "We both know this won't last."

Dell scooted forward in his chair. "I promise to be the best you I can be, Dad."

Their father shook his head again. "Nope. Because you're not me, but you are a great you. I pray you won't be me in the end."

Nora fought back a sob in her throat. How many times would she grieve her father and all he was leaving behind?

Dad had wanted to look at the space Nora would use for a studio before they returned to the home. Nora pointed out what she planned to do, never taking her eyes off her father.

They rejoined Dell a little while later in his office.

Their father frowned at the space.

"This used to be … used to be just storage, I think." He looked at Dell who nodded.

"We moved all that stuff upstairs when you hired me, remember?"

Nora nudged him with her elbow and whispered, "No, you dolt."

Dell cringed. "Sorry. I … forgot." He cleared his throat. "Anyway, you didn't want that stuff in the basement due to the possible dampness."

Nora thought again about the two rooms full of boxes upstairs. They should start going through those files soon. Maybe some items could be given to the local historical society or simply scanned into digital files. She was unsure what really lay up there, untouched for who knew how long.

Her father now looked at her intently. "Don't just throw everything out."

She nodded, and he continued into the main parlor.

"I often thought about expanding," he said as he looked up at the ceiling and the walls still covered with Victorian wallpaper. "We don't have enough room on this lot, but maybe …" He paused, as if the thought had simply fled from his brain. Nora didn't press, but just watched silently.

"You've mentioned that to me," Dell said. "Nora and I can talk more about that, but I think this building is an important landmark to the people of this town."

Their father nodded. "Pulpit goes here." He pointed and Nora nodded even though she knew this basic information. "And coffin or urn display here."

"I know, Dad."

He gazed at her for a long minute before walking back toward the front of the house. "I guess we should get me back to the asylum," he said. "They're probably losing their minds over there." He stopped short and turned back to Nora and Dell. "No pun intended."

She smiled. "None taken. And Dell already called them."

Their father nodded, then continued his walk toward the front door. Once there, he reached out and touched the stained-glass window inlaid in the door. "You said Bud is dead?"

Nora looked at Dell, who grimaced. Would they ever get used to the constant memory loss? "Yes, Dad. He died the other day. He hadn't been well."

"I would like to come to the funeral." He turned to her with raised eyebrows. "Can I?"

Nora nodded. "Of course, Dad. I'll be sure you're here. Bud would have liked that. Others will like it."

He made a sound with his throat but said nothing more.

Chapter Twenty-seven

That next Saturday, Nora stood at the front door welcoming many people into Bud Hoffmaster's funeral. Sarah had come earlier to see that everything was as Bud wanted and to set up photos from his life. Most prominent on the display were the most recent ones Nora had taken of the family.

Luke came up to her during a small break in the line. He looked dashing in his gray Brooks Brothers suit with pale blue tie that accentuated his eye color.

"I'm sorry for just showing up the other day and being a wreck."

She accepted his apology with a smile. "Forgotten. Grief makes us do some weird things."

Luke nodded and sighed. "Maybe I could make it up to you by buying you dinner."

A couple walked through the door, and Nora greeted them as Luke stepped aside. They shook his hand next before moving to the guest book.

"When are you heading back?" Nora said when the couple had entered the parlor.

Luke shoved his hands into his pants pockets, the bottom of his suit jacket bunching up. "I'm not sure. I've really liked being here with Sarah and the kids. And Brian is okay too." He winked. "I can do a lot of things remotely."

Nora fought the urge to press him for anything. If he stayed or left meant nothing to her. Although she needed to focus more on her father and her business, especially getting the upstairs room ready for family portraits, Luke was handsome, and she wouldn't mind spending some time with him.

Luke shrugged. "Maybe I'll buy a house and start a life here. Taxes are certainly cheaper, and I know my funeral will be well taken care of."

Nora laughed as the tension left her shoulders. "That's true."

"What do you say? Dinner sometime?"

Nora shrugged. "Sure. Sarah has my number."

Luke smiled and nodded. "Do you plan to start your own photography business?" he asked.

She nodded. "I do. I'm renovating an upstairs room into a studio."

"You're not going to get rid of the fancy red globed lamps, right? I mean ... those just scream comfort and sophistication."

A burst of laughter bubbled out, and she immediately covered her mouth with her hand.

Luke squeezed her elbow as another group walked in the door. He greeted them before returning to his family at the front of the parlor.

Nora guided the newcomers into the room, pointing out the guestbook and the funeral cards. When she turned, Mrs. Cipriani stood before her leaning on her cane.

"Mrs. C, how nice to see you." Nora leaned in to give the old woman a peck on the cheek.

"Hello, Nora. Yes. I knew Bud a little bit but wanted to come and support you as well. Calvin brought me and is waiting in the car."

Nora thought this must be what her father had meant when he said he cared about the people of this town. It wasn't hard to see the way people interconnected when so many passed by your station to bring condolences to people they may have only known for a season. Millsburgh was a town full of small connections, but each one left lasting impressions. Maybe that would be the name of her business ... Lasting Impressions.

"Is your father here?" Mrs. C asked.

Nora nodded. "Yes." She pointed him out in the crowd of people waiting for the service to start. He sat next to Dell with Natalie on the other side, a protective wall, they hoped, to keep him in one spot today. "He was semi-coherent this morning," she told Mrs. C, "but he goes in and out."

"Yes, his memory will be that way now." Mrs. C reached out to touch her arm. "Be thankful for every moment you can have of clarity."

"I agree. When he ran the other day, I was so afraid I would never see him again. You hear so many horror stories. But he was the most lucid I have seen him in a long time for a good amount of time." She turned to look at Mrs. C. "But when he lost the thoughts again ..."

Mrs. C nodded. "It's hard. Enjoy every moment."

More folks came into the home, and Nora directed them to the guestbook and inside the parlor. Then she gently pulled Mrs. C away from the front door.

"Did I tell you I found a place for my photography studio? Just upstairs. That way I can be here and still help Dell while also running my business."

"Oh, how wonderful. This building is so beautiful. Look at this ornate detail on that banister." She smoothed her wrinkled hand over the woodwork with a loving touch. "People will love getting the photos done with these surroundings."

Nora agreed. "According to my dad, my great-grandfather carved some of this banister himself. He was an amateur woodworker."

"Then you get your creative talents naturally." Mrs. C smiled at her.

"I never thought of that, but I guess."

More people came in, and Nora pointed them in the right direction with a smile. She turned back to Mrs. C. "I truly feel like I have found the purpose God wants for me here. This place always just felt like death to me. Sadness and misery. But now there's ..."

"Life," said Mrs. C.

Nora nodded. "I was going to say hope, but yes. Life. I pray it'll give people hope and life in the midst of their grieving."

Mrs. C tapped her cane on the dark wood floor a few times, as if contemplating her reply. "When my Sal died, I quit painting or doing anything creative for a long time. The grief was too great. But one day, I walked past an art supply store and decided to go in. The smell, the displays, the fun, new products sparked something within again. I bought a small canvas and a simple paint set with brushes. I went home and painted." She looked into Nora's eyes. "And I felt light again. Like the grief was less. Like I could go on. You see"—she tapped her cane again on the floor as if to accentuate her point—"God gives us coping skills, Nora. We sometimes think they're frivolous or just a hobby. But these gifts God gives are meant to enrich our lives and the lives of others. If we stop using them ... what do you think happens?"

Nora felt as if she were once again in Mrs. C's classroom. "I don't know. I guess ... based on your story, we have trouble getting over things?"

Mrs. C waved her hand. "Obedience, dear. We stop being obedient to God. Let me ask you something, was I a good teacher?"

"Oh yes. I loved your classes. I learned to love art and figured out I had some talent at doing it."

"Okay. Good." Mrs. C smiled at her. "Do you think you might have missed out on that if I hadn't been your teacher? If you hadn't taken an art class?"

Nora thought about the question for a moment. She would need to start the service soon, but this conversation felt too important. "Yes. I think I might not have realized my skill."

"I think God would have brought you to this gift eventually, but"—she held up one finger—"I think I would have not been obedient on my part to help you if I hadn't become a teacher. You see I had two callings. One to create art and one to teach. You might not have felt like this funeral home was part of your purpose, yet you can add in your talent here. You can use all the gifts God has given you to make this place your own. Your brother too. And you can continue to be obedient in what God calls you to do while also using that gift he has given you to find rest, comfort, peace within yourself."

"I never thought about things in those terms before."

"You certainly brought comfort with your skills."

Nora thought about the photo shoot with the Hoffmasters and smiled. The experience had been just as beneficial to her as it had to them. She had felt light, free when taking the photos. She had enjoyed watching the kids interact with the adults and how Bud's face had shone with love for his family.

"Thanks, Mrs. C. You have given me a lot to think about." Nora looked at the clock. "I need to start the service. Can I help you to a seat?"

After the service, Nora stood to the side as people conversed for a few moments before heading to a meal at a local restaurant. The family had opted not to go to the graveside today, which made Nora's life easier. Dell had taken Dad back to the home with Natalie and the kids before the end of the service to avoid Dad becoming overwhelmed. She would meet Dell and his family there to have lunch together—even with the kids—instead of the Hoffmasters.

Nora loved the mix of tears and smiles. Bud had obviously affected many people in many ways. Many gathered around the photo boards set up in the parlor. Sarah's mother had lingered over the pictures for a long time, touching some and pointing many out to those gathered.

Sarah approached her with another woman Nora didn't know.

"Nora, I'd like you to meet Beth Wilson. She and her family moved here about five years ago, and they go to our church."

"Nice to meet you, Beth." Nora held out her hand and the two shook.

"Sarah pointed out the photos you took before Bud passed. I was wondering if you do that as a side job or ..."

"I kind of just did those as a favor to Sarah. Although I'm setting up a photography studio upstairs here, but I'm not quite ready yet."

"She's very talented," Sarah said, putting her arm through the crook of Nora's elbow and pulling her close.

"I love the photos," Beth said. "I was wondering if you might do something similar for my family. My mom is in declining health, and we're not sure how much longer we might have. You could simply come to our house like you did Sarah."

Nora nodded. "Of course. I would be happy to."

"Sarah said you didn't charge her, but I must pay you. I believe in supporting artists, and you deserve money for your time and talents."

Nora started to protest but thought of Mrs. C's talk from earlier. God had given her this gift and perhaps he meant for this to be an added value to the business, not just for her own benefit. What had Mrs. C said? Two *callings*.

"Okay. Let me know when would work for you."

Beth smiled. "I'll get your number from Sarah later. Today is their day. But thank you for introducing us, Sarah."

Beth touched Sarah's elbow and offered one of those "I'm so sorry" smiles before walking away.

Nora noticed the smile slip away from Sarah's face as her friend walked away.

"Tired?" Nora asked her. "Do you want us to move people along?"

Nora knew people often lingered for too long when the bereaved wanted time alone or when they simply wanted to finish up the day.

Sarah nodded. "I think we need to move on. The kids are tired, and we still have the luncheon." She turned to Nora. "Thank you for all you've done. Bud would have loved this day. Please join us at the luncheon. Dell and his family too."

Nora shook her head. "We're having lunch with Dad back at Ravensbridge. Things were getting too overwhelming for him here. But I can make an announcement to those still lingering and help you pack up what you need."

Brian walked up to them and put his arm around Sarah's waist, kissing her on the temple. "Ready?"

Nora stepped back into her funeral director role as she announced the Hoffmasters would like everyone to move on to the restaurant for the luncheon. When everyone but the family was left, she stood aside as they said their last goodbyes to Bud. When they were done, she helped them pack up flowers and the photo display and ushered them to their cars.

Sarah put down her car window as they began to pull away. "Sure you don't want lunch with us?"

Nora shook her head. "No, thanks. But we can get together soon? Lunch, just the two of us? Or I can introduce you to my friend Jill."

Sarah waved as they made their way down the street.

Nora watched them go, feeling happy to have made some new friends even in the midst of such a sad time.

Chapter Twenty-eight

The next day Nora sat next to Natalie and her niece Katie at the Millsburgh Baptist Church for their 10:10 a.m. service. Dell sat at the end with the other boys between him and his wife.

Little Katie leaned into her arm, and Nora looked down at the girl's sweet face.

"Aunt Nora, I need a 'nack."

"A what, baby?"

"A 'nack. Da little fishies." Katie mimed putting food into her mouth.

"Oh, I don't—"

"Katie," Natalie hissed. "You just had breakfast. You don't need a snack." Nora's sister-in-law looked at her and fought to keep a smile from her face. When Katie focused her attention back on her dolly, Natalie opened her purse for only Nora to see. Inside were several packs of cheddar flavored snacks. Natalie winked and put a finger up to her lips in a shushing motion.

Nora grinned and put her arm around her niece, hugging her tight.

She loved that coming to church was a time she could spend with her loved ones. If she'd ever moved away, she would have missed that.

She saw Jill come in, and she waved. Her friend walked over with a smile.

"Fancy seeing you here, stranger. You owe me another lunch. How's your dad?"

"He's doing okay. Settling into Ravensbridge. He's made a few friends. My old art teacher lives there too."

"Fabulous. I'm glad he's adjusting." She waved a hand at Dell and his family before focusing back on Nora. "Lunch this week?"

"Totally. I'll text you. I might invite Sarah, Bud Hoffmaster's granddaughter. You'll like her."

"Sounds great. I'd love to meet her." She wiggled her fingers in a wave and went to sit with her husband a few pews in front of them.

The piano music ended, and the worship leader came to the pulpit. After giving an opening Scripture and leading the congregation in a few hymns, he sat, and Pastor Richfield took his place at the pulpit.

"Good morning. I'm so glad you're here today." He paused as members of the crowd echoed his greetings. "I was so glad to see many of you yesterday at Bud Hoffmaster's funeral. I know his family appreciated your attendance and well wishes as they move forward without their patriarch. Bud was so instrumental in helping this church grow. I'm glad that his granddaughter Sarah and her family are now coming regularly." He nodded to where Sarah and Brian sat with their kids. "If you weren't able to go yesterday, please be sure and say a word to them today after service."

Pastor Richfield led the congregation in prayer and began his sermon.

"Today we're going to be looking at Romans 8:28 which says, 'And we know that all things work together for good to them that love God, to them who are the called according to his purpose.'

"We hear this verse misconstrued as a 'God is going to give me everything I want' kind of thing. God is *so* good and loves me *so* much that he is going to just bless me over and over again like some kind of fun lottery."

Several people in the congregation chuckled.

"But I don't think Bud's loved ones or the Harper family who are dealing with a father who has dementia think they are being blessed by God right now."

Nora sat up straighter in the pew.

"But it's that one little word in this Scripture that always gets me. All. It's right there at the beginning, so how do we miss it? How do we not understand that even in the suffering, even in the heartache, even in the sorrow, God is working *all* things out for our good? *All* things. Have you ever gone through something difficult in your life and thought, 'What good could come of this?' And then ... something good comes. Life-threatening diagnoses often lead to repentance, salvation. Grief often draws us closer to God. Helps us focus where maybe we weren't focused before—on the things God wants us to do. Sarah and her family moved here to help Bud at the end of his life, and now they want to stay. They've found family, friends, and purpose here. Sarah's mother repaired her relationship with her father before he died. All things lead to good when it's in the Father's hands."

The pastor elaborated more as Nora sat stunned by this bit of revelation. All things ... even her father's dementia? She thought more on this as the pastor continued. If her dad hadn't been forced to quit working at the funeral home, would she have gone on working more dead-end jobs, never finding her own purpose? Had God been working things out this entire time? She thought of Mrs. C at the nursing home. God knew she needed some sign that moving her dad there would be okay. Had God been working all this time to that end?

Nora let each thing Pastor Richfield said sink into her soul. She had been tossed about, trying to find her own way all this time, and yet God had been working on her behalf. To work everything out for his purposes. Not *her* purposes. *His*. Every season she had tried to start fresh, had tried to make her own way, had sought some kind of niche in which to fit, but she hadn't turned to the one source who had been working hard for her—God.

The funeral home was a ministry to the people of Millsburgh, not some frightening horror house. Something needed in the darkest of days. The business wasn't just about being efficient and making money. Running their business with God's purposes in mind meant showing up for people at their homes, providing options so they could choose, but also helping them to choose and not taking advantage of them when they were grieving. Yes, the funeral home relied on the deaths of others, but also provided gifts to the living.

And now the added benefit of family photos would benefit both the business and the grieving. A bit of hope and light they could look back on to help them with their grief.

When the sermon and last hymn concluded, Nora hugged her family and walked out of the church with a new purpose in mind.

An hour later, Nora walked along a nature path on the outskirts of town. The trail meandered through some wooded forest as well as along the edge of a farmer's field. She walked over a small wooden bridge, stopping to snap a couple of pictures as she went. The quiet stillness of the place filled her heart with peace and calm, unlike any she had felt for a long while.

A small bug crawled along the wooden railing, and she bent down to take its picture. She might need to invest in a different lens to take some macro photography. She wondered if she could make money from that but decided to let God work out that part.

She pulled her coat closer as she walked the path, leaves crunching beneath her feet. She loved the smell of autumn in Pennsylvania—the crisp tang of molding leaves. A breeze fluttered the trees above and she snapped another photo of the towering oaks. A small stream trickled beneath her. She stopped to take another pic of some small minnows within the gurgling water.

A bench beckoned ahead, and Nora took long strides to get to it. She put down the camera and closed her eyes, enjoying the sounds alone.

The ping of her phone caused her to open her eyes. She swiped open her phone to see a text from Gabe.

GABE: Sorry I've been AWOL. Do you have time to chat?

A moment later she was talking to her new friend from her time in the Outer Banks.

"Are things calming down now?" he asked.

"Yes, somewhat. I'll begin renovations on the upstairs room next week. Renovating should go quickly. I just need to clean and add a coat of paint to the walls. I think something bright to lighten up the place. That will help until I can afford a light stand."

"It's good to hear hope in your voice. You sound like the Nora I met at the beach again."

Nora agreed. Hearing Gabe's voice felt like talking to a really old friend.

"How's Gladys?" she asked.

"She's okay. The new business is going well. We have some remodeling to do too, but we already have several local groups interested in using the space after hours. That will help bring in some much-needed funds."

Nora listened as Gabe outlined the changes at the coffee shop. She realized God had been working in Gabe's life for his good too.

"You've come a long way in a year," she told him.

There was a moment of quiet on his end before he simply said, "Yeah."

"I've been taking more photos," she told him. "I'll text you a few of some scenery that I took here just now."

"Are you going to do some art shows with your photography?"

She hadn't thought about that just yet, but the desire to do so was strong. As if now that she'd dug into this gift, God was showing her new and exciting ways she could use it. She'd been visiting Mrs. C every time she saw her dad and had even taken one of her painting classes. Now that she had awakened her creative spirit, she couldn't get enough. She was thankful she'd run into her old art teacher that first trip.

Another thing you were working on, huh, Lord?

Nora closed her eyes again and felt the breeze on her skin. When she heard Gabe clear his throat, she realized she'd missed what he'd said.

"I'm sorry. I was lost in my own little world here for a minute. What did you say?"

"I'll be coming to PA to visit some family around the holidays. I was wondering if maybe I could see you."

Nora looked at her camera's viewfinder for a moment, flipping through the last several photos she had taken and feeling a certain peace in her soul. "I'd like that. But can we be clear about being just friends? I'm not ready for anything ... relationship related."

Although she had agreed to dinner with Luke.

"I understand. You're kind of like another sister to me anyway."

She laughed. "That grotesque, huh?" Gabe stuttered and stumbled until she said, "Just a joke. I'm kidding. Friends joke around, ya know."

"You're a very beautiful woman."

"Stop. Just friends, remember?" Gabe offered his assent, and she continued, "My dad's situation might be a kink in any plans for your trip. It's very day by day with him, and Dell and I are trying to be sure we don't forget about him." *The way his disease has forced him to forget us.* "There's a bit of grieving I'm going through too."

"Well, good thing you have a friend now who understands that."

Nora smiled. "I look forward to seeing you then, Gabe, my new friend."

They chatted a few more moments, making plans to touch base again. Gabe promised to let her know when he could visit, and she promised to have Natalie cook for him while he was in town.

When she'd clicked off the conversation, she sat in silence for a bit.

Tap, tap, tap.

She squinted up at the tree looming into the sky across from her, using her hand to shield the sun from her eyes.

Tap, tap, tap.

A woodpecker.

She found the little bird's even smaller patch of red among the branches in the tree and raised her camera. She snapped off several photos, using different adjustments and zoom features to capture the best photo. After checking the viewfinder to see she'd captured what she'd intended, she sat back and let the day pass around her.

Eventually Nora rose, the chill of the late afternoon seeping into her bones. She took pictures as she made her way back to her car.

Nora wondered if perhaps she could find some kind of nature photography group or class. Or maybe she should start one of her own. That would bring extra money in too and she could—

She stopped in the middle of the path and looked up to the sky.

"Oops. Getting ahead of myself again, aren't I, God?" She laughed. "How about I just let you lead for a while?"

A gentle breeze brushed past her cheeks as Nora stepped forward with the assurance that God was already working out every new purpose that might come her way.

About the Author

Sue A. Fairchild has had many jobs, both creative (graphic designer) and not (insurance agent), but when she sold that first devotion in 2012, her whole life changed. Now she claims the titles of writer, editor, writing coach, webmistress, and speaker and has helped a variety of authors get their manuscripts into readers' hands. She loves working with clients who are working toward the greater good of sharing God's message in this world. And she hopes her stories do the same.

Visit Sue's website here: https://sueafairchild.wordpress.com and the links to her books here: https://sueafairchild.wordpress.com/social/

If you're an author, sign up for her free newsletter for writers (https://tinyurl.com/mrxb9fmf), or visit her Instagram page: @suefairchildedits

Discussion Questions:

1. Nora struggles with her worth, especially when it comes to her family's funeral home business and finding her place there. How can you relate to Nora in this aspect?

2. Do you think Nora and Jake should have given their relationship one more try, or do you think she was right in letting it go?

3. There are multiple themes going on in this book—loss of relationships, caregiving, discovering your God-given gifts, familial bonds, and understanding God's purpose for your life. Which one(s) do you most relate to and why?

4. Think about the relationship between Nora and her brother Dell. Do you see similarities to your own familial relationships? Discuss.

5. Nora has a very adverse reaction to moving her father to the nursing home. Do you or your family have similar aversions and, if so, why?

6. Discuss the conception that nursing homes are "bad" places for the elderly. Where does this idea come from? If you don't think they are "bad" places, discuss why.

7. Nora learns new ways of interacting with her father through the nurse's aide that comes to their house. What new things did you learn from this section of the book?

8. If you have ever been a caregiver for someone with dementia or Alzheimer's, talk with your group about your experience or journal the things that helped you during that time. Perhaps find a local organization to provide your experience with. It might help someone else experiencing a similar situation.

9. Who do you turn to most often when you need support? Make a list of these people and give them thanks.

10. Nora struggles with knowing God's purpose for her life, but she knows some of her talents. If you're trying to understand your purpose, make a list of things you're good at or enjoy doing, then pray over each and listen for God's voice.

11. Between Gabe, Jake, and Luke, which man do you think is the best fit for Nora and why? Or should she hold out for someone else?

Support Resources

**Find help for those you love
with these organizations:**

Alzheimer's Support

Alzheimer's Association - www.alz.org/help-support/i-have-alz/programs-support

Alzheimer 24/7 Helpline – 1.800.272.3900

Alzheimers.gov

Alzheimer's Foundation of America - alzfdn.org/

Caregiver Support

National Council on Aging - www.ncoa.org/caregivers/benefits/caregiver-support

AARP - https://www.aarp.org/caregiving/

National Institute on Aging - https://www.nia.nih.gov/health/caregiving

Also check with your local churches, Salvation Army, or the American Red Cross for additional organizations, programs, and communities that serve those dealing with eldercare or Alzheimer's issues.

Sue's Award-Winning Book

www.ingramcontent.com/pod-product-compliance
Lightning Source LLC
Chambersburg PA
CBHW051133020726
47501CB00005B/1486